Hi Everyone,

It's always fun to find a new Christmas romance – and always fun to write one!

Star is a great character to spend time with, quirky, resilient, independent and just plain fun.

She first appeared in Home for Christmas, when she thought Blue might be the reason fate had brought her to Fortune Bay, but then bowed out gracefully when it became clear he had to work things out with Louise.

Star became more entrenched in the community in Starting Over, becoming friends with Lily and saving Marshall from the paparazzi at the Fishing Derby.

Consequently, when I finished writing Starting Over, I felt that Starlight was unfinished business. While everyone else had gotten to live in the cabin, Star was stuck in Blue's cold drafty apartment at the station. And although it wasn't always what they thought they were looking for, they'd all found their happily-ever-after there.

So surely it was Star's turn! And who better to pair her up with in her own story than her exact opposite, buttoned-down Harry Brewster, Marshall's L.A. agent.

Thanks to my daughter Rosey Hudson for her help, as always, with the cover and, yoga retreat aficionado that she is, for the idea of yoga instructor as a career path for our sweetly counter-culture Star.

Thanks to my friend and editor Stephanie Webb for always being there to talk over plot points, and for adding so much to this book. And to Ann and Susheela for the proofreads.

I hope you enjoy reading Starlight and Tinsel as much as I enjoyed writing it.

Thanks for reading Fortune Bay books.

Judy Hudson

Starlight and Tinsel

A Fortune Bay Novella

by

Judith Hudson

Chapter 1

* * * * * * *

Star packed the last heavy box into her old VW van and slid the side door shut. She and her mom had named it Eden because of the painting of Adam and Eve, in all their naked glory, on the side. Her mother had left Eden to her when she died, and in a strange way Star felt that through the beat-up old van, they were still connected. Like her mother was watching out for her from the other side, guiding her journey.

So, when Eden conked out a year ago to the day, right here in this workshop parking lot where there just happened to be a tiny apartment waiting for her, well, she felt it was meant to be.

A snowflake tingled on her nose. It had been snowing the night Eden had brought her to Fortune Bay, too. That dark blowy night, she'd thought Blue's workshop was still a gas station, as indeed it had been years ago when the mill was running and Fortune Bay was a thriving sawmill town. It was cold that night too, when her van had puffed its final breath.

Star knew serendipity when she saw it and had thought, for a while at least, that Blue might be the one. The reason she'd been led to Fortune Bay. But then Louise came back to town and in a flash, Star saw that he wasn't the one. Not her one, anyway. She still wasn't sure just why she'd landed here, but there must be a reason. She'd stay until she figured it out, then she and Eden would hit the road again.

She waited by the van, tugging her rainbow leg warmers up over her knees and pulling the fingers of her convertible mittens over her fingertips. Such a great idea, these knit mittens with the fingertip pouch that you could pull off, but that stayed attached to the gloves until you needed them. More trouble to knit, but definitely worth the effort. She was sure they'd be a hit at the Fortune Bay Christmas craft show later this month.

Stamping her feet to keep the blood circulating, she tucked her hands under her arms to hold in the warmth. She was kind of sorry to be leaving the old Station. Her friend and landlord Blue still worked in the attached garage bays that he'd converted into a woodworking shop and, although quiet, Blue was a nice guy and they had a relaxed relationship. He'd turned the old office and convenience store into a small—very small—apartment years ago, but the cabin she was moving to today was bigger and hopefully warmer. She was surprised by the excitement she felt to be moving there. She usually only felt this kind of rush when she was moving on to another town. Obviously, she wasn't finished with Fortune Bay yet.

A tow truck pulled into the lot. Star waved to the driver and Lorne lifted a hand in reply. He backed the truck up to the van, climbed out of the cab and loosened the big hook.

"I could fix this, you know. You could pay me a bit at a time." He cast a glance in her direction. "We could work something out."

Lorne was nice, but he was still a guy, and she had an idea what the terms of that deal might be. A regular at the café where she worked, she knew he was divorced and lonely. "Thanks, Lorne, but I think I'll wait. I'll have the money together soon."

"Okay then. Put 'er in neutral."

Star climbed into Eden, shifted into neutral, eased off the brake and hopped out of the van. The winch on the tow truck groaned and creaked as the Eden's front end lifted off the ground.

"Hop in," Lorne said as he climbed back into the cab of the truck.

Sure, hop in, she thought as she clambered up—way up—into the cab. These things weren't built for someone like her, someone who was five foot two. Okay, five foot one, but claiming that extra inch did wonders for her self-esteem.

The tow truck rumbled to life and started the slow drive through Fortune Bay: past the four streets of little crayon-colored houses that had been built by the mill long ago for its workers, past the park and the Hall, past the general store and the café where she worked, across the bridge and out of town. *Her town.* She'd been here for a year and it was beginning to feel like her town. Weird.

"How you going to get to work?" Lorne asked, eyes on the road.

"It's not that far. I'll figure out something."

He was right, though. The cabin was farther from the store and café than Blue's workshop had been, and the weather was getting steadily worse. But still, it was only about a mile. Except in the worst weather, she could probably hike it. The walk would do her good. Or hitch. In a town like Fortune Bay, odds were, she'd know everyone who'd drive by. That was the upside of working at the café—even though she'd only lived here for a year, she knew everyone in town.

The downside was, well, working at the café. It was the longest she'd ever stuck to one job, and slinging breakfasts and burgers was not on her top ten list of dream jobs. But there wasn't a lot of choice in a town of less than a thousand souls—and even that was up from nine hundred since the resort opened last spring. New people were flooding into town, and that was kind of exciting to watch happen. Almost made her feel like a local.

The road followed the shore of Majestic Lake, and here and there she caught glimpses of the dark stormy water through the trees. The snow started coming down more insistently, wet flakes splatting against the windshield as they passed the old log farmhouse set back from the road. Then they turned down the dark, tree-shrouded lane to the cabin, Lorne easing the van carefully over the potholes in the dirt road. Big flakes the size of nickels hit the windscreen and created a lacy coating of snow on the fir branches that met overhead.

At the sight of the building, she felt excitement stir in the air. Star had always felt the cabin was a special place, had felt it when she'd visited her friend Lily there and, before that, Louise. She couldn't help noticing that, as if enchanted, everyone who lived in the cabin seemed to find their happily-ever-after. Not always exactly what they were expecting, but, in the end, just what they wanted.

The thought that it might be her turn both scared and excited her. She just hoped she didn't do something stupid to break the spell now that she was living here. And she could—she knew she could—without even trying. Her life never seemed to be entirely under her control, but she'd learned long ago to put a smile on her face and make the best of it. She was alive, healthy, and still young. Anything could happen.

"Just park it there, behind the shed," she said.

"Going to be pretty chilly inside," Lorne said, his eyes on the side mirror as he expertly backed the VW into the spot. "I could help you warm it up." He flicked a glance in her direction.

She laughed. "Good try. I managed in Blue's shop all last winter." It had been cold all right, but not as cold as spending the winter in the van. And she'd done that too. She could manage a woodstove as well as the next guy. Had been doing it off and on all her life.

Before Lorne had gotten Eden's front tires back on the ground, she'd climbed down out of the cab. "I see a bit of firewood stacked there against the house. I'll be fine."

When the winch was secured to the back of the truck, she counted out the agreed upon fee and handed it over.

"Well, you give me a call if you need anything. And remember what I said about those repairs. I didn't mean anything funny about that."

"I know you didn't, Lorne. And thanks. I'll remember." *Now please, just leave.* She couldn't wait to get inside, but didn't want Lorne to follow her in. She didn't have a lot of things in this life, but her privacy was one thing she valued.

Adam and Eve slid aside as she opened the side door of the van and hauled out the first of her boxes.

As he pulled away, Lorne called out the window, "I could help you carry your boxes in."

She kept on walking. "Got it. Thanks." Soon the tow truck chugged away down the driveway, and then—silence.

Stopping at the top of the porch steps, she took a moment to savor the solitude. Blue's was pretty quiet, but she'd still heard sounds of traffic going to and from the village. This was different. This was deep-in-the-woods-with-falling-snow quiet. She took a deep breath. The faintly metallic, musky smell was invigorating, and, with a smile, she turned to go inside.

The front door flew open before she reached it and Lily appeared, a grin on her face and her arms spread wide. "Welcome."

Lily's twelve-year-old step-son Boz pushed past her and mimicked her gesture. "It's your new home. There's a ghost!"

"Take the box," Lily suggested, and he scooped the box out of Star's hands, almost bowling her over with his enthusiasm. Boz was a big kid, already bigger than Star, and rapidly outgrowing his baby-fat years. He disappeared inside with the box.

"Let's help Star with the rest of the boxes," Lily called over her shoulder as she started down the steps. They trooped out to the van and Star reached for the side-door handle, nestled between Eve's voluptuous breasts, which were barely covered by the proverbial fig leaf. When Boz's cheeks burst into flame, she shot Lily a grin.

"So, the cabin is haunted," she said, breaking Boz's rapt concentration on the couple on the door by putting a big box into his waiting arms. "Did anything happen when you lived here, Lily?"

"I did notice a few things," Lily said as they walked past the periwinkle shutters and silvered wood siding back to the porch. "I moved in last summer right when Dorothy was moving out. Dorothy was Augusta's sister—Augusta's the ghost, by the way—and they seemed to talk all the time. At first, I thought Dorothy was a bit batty, she is getting on, but then there were the other things..."

"Like what?" They piled the boxes on the living room rug and headed back out for another load.

"Well, Augusta seems to be sort of a matchmaker. Or at least she tries to nudge you along. Out of your relationship comfort zone."

Star gave her a skeptically amused glance as they loaded up again. "Really?"

"Really. She liked to pick out my clothes when I was going on a date and, well, she seemed to speak to me, inside my head..." She sent Star a sideways glance. "Sound crazy?"

Star shook her head. "No." This was nothing compared to the hocus pocus her mother believed permeated the world.

Lily laughed. "Well, at the time *I* often questioned my sanity." She walked into the cabin and over to a photograph on the wall by the back stairs. "This is Augusta. Maddie found the negative and developed this photograph when she lived here a couple of years ago."

Star walked over and studied the black and white photograph of a young woman, waving out the driver's window of a car with a split front windscreen, an exuberant smile on her face. Star grinned. "Well, hello Augusta."

Lily looked around the cabin. "I'll sort of miss her. But onward and upward." They stepped back out onto the porch. "I'd better get back. We still have a lot of unpacking to do. It's been quite the week, seems like everyone in town has moved one door to the left. Harry—you remember Harry Brewster, you met him last summer—well, he and Marshall are making dinner. I'm not sure what to expect."

Marshall was Lily's new significant other and Harry was his former—maybe present, Star wasn't sure—agent. She pressed her lips together, then said, "Harry's visiting?"

"He's up from L.A. for a while. He and Marshall are looking for a place they can turn into a recording studio. Marsh is hoping Harry will stay and help him run it. Marshall's committed to staying in Fortune Bay, but I'm afraid Harry is still on the fence."

Star had met Harry a few times last summer but didn't know what to think about him. Not that she had to think anything, but he stuck out like a sore thumb in Fortune Bay with his pressed chinos and shiny city shoes.

"How long is he staying?"

"Harry?" Lily wiggled her eyebrows. "Why? You interested?"

Star laughed. "No. I mean, he's a good-looking guy—"

"And rich."

"I guess. That's never very important to me."

Lily grinned. "It is nice, though." Then she sobered. "But you're right, we can all see, after what happened to Marshall, that money doesn't always ensure happiness."

"You guys are happy now, though, aren't you?"

"Yes," Lily said emphatically. "But Marsh had a pretty rough time after the accident. I don't know what would have happened to him if it hadn't been for Harry. He did everything for Marsh and the kids."

"He looks..." Remembering his pressed shorts and polo shirts, Star searched for a word that wouldn't sound like a put-down. "Dependable."

"He's been devoted to Marshall since they were kids.

Now, I think, he's kind of at loose ends. Harry always helped with the family before, but now Marsh has me. And Marshall's career has changed tracks, they are no longer touring with the band and the show, and that was something Harry always took care of. He doesn't really have a role here, and when he goes back to L.A. he doesn't really have a place in that scene anymore either."

"Can we go now?" Boz asked, jumping up on the porch.

"Sure," Lilly said, and Boz raced down the steps and up the lane.

A blast of wind blew in off the lake and Star shivered. "I should check the fire. Thanks for starting it."

"Boz wanted to learn, but it was just kindling so it probably needs some bigger pieces of wood by now. There are a few good chunks inside."

"Great. Want to come in for a coffee?"

"Tempting, but I'd better get back. Why don't you come for dinner?"

Star thought about the scant rations she had brought from the Station. "That would be great."

"Okay. Come at five. It's just the family."

When Lily disappeared around the corner of the cabin, Star turned once again to the door. The screen door stood open, but the wooden inside door was firmly closed. She turned the knob, but the door wouldn't budge. Locked. Seriously? They'd just been going in and out with her boxes. She put her hip to the panel and thumped, but it didn't budge. Standing back, she jiggled the handle—and the door silently drifted open. Her eyes dropped to the floor, and a voice in her head whispered the words printed on the mat just inside the door. *"Welcome home."*

She grinned. Haunted. This was going to be fun.

Chapter 2
✳ ✳ ✳ ✳ ✳ ✳

They had piled her boxes on the floor in the kitchen side of the big main room. The living room area occupied the right-hand side and was designated by a faded Persian rug. Placed around the carpet was a big old couch and chair set, the velvet arms worn thin from years of use. She pushed the furniture back until it hit the walls and with a feeling of deep relief, lay down on her back on the carpet.

She stretched as long as her five-foot-one-inches would stretch, then longer still with her arms reaching above her head. She swung them wide until she was as big as she could possibly be and thrilled that still she didn't touch the edges of the thick carpet. Paradise. How long had it been since she'd had a place to do yoga? There hadn't been room at Blue's apartment to do more than curl up in a child's pose. And in the van, it was out of the question.

She'd spent the summer before she arrived at Fortune Bay working in the canteen of a spa on the California coast where she'd made healthy smoothies and indulged in as many classes a day as her schedule would allow. She had racked up quite a few hours towards her instructor's certificate that summer but still needed twenty more and could use a few other courses before she'd feel truly qualified to teach. But this—she lifted her hips into a Bridge Pose, *Setu Bandha Sarvangasana*—this was pure bliss.

Exhaling a long breath, she sat up and faced the kitchen. Getting to her feet, she hurried over to check the cupboards and heaved a sigh of relief to find Lily had left the china dishes. Star hadn't thought to ask if the kitchen came fully equipped, but thank the Buddha it did, because she didn't have any kitchen equipment of her own except for her hexagonal, stovetop espresso maker. She'd spent half a year working at a Starbucks in Seattle and liked her coffee the way she'd learned to make it there. Strong.

Through the kitchen window Star could see the snow still coming down, big wet flakes piling up on the porch railing. The cabin was still cold, and a shiver wiggled her shoulders. In the stove, the fire had almost burned away so she put in a few more pieces of cedar on top, along with a larger split log. She'd have to source some dry wood soon if she planned to stay the winter and see about doing some winterizing.

If there was one thing she knew, it was how to tighten up leaky old buildings. The board ceiling suggested no insulation above, but a trap door at the top of the rough staircase at the back of the kitchen gave easy access to the attic. She could talk to Stephanie Murphy, her landlady, about throwing down some insulation up there. Maybe even pour some loose fill down the walls if they were open from above. She'd do the labor in return for rent if Stephanie bought the material. And she'd definitely get some insulating window film to cut the drafts. The fresh logs caught and soon the fire was blazing. It would be fine. Cozy. Paradise, in fact. A job and her own place to live? What more could she ask?

Swinging the door of the woodstove shut with a clang, she turned to her boxes. She traveled light but had learned long ago how to make a temporary accommodation feel like home.

First, she put her expresso maker on the kitchen counter beside the turquoise stove. An old beauty, Lily said most of the pushbutton burners still worked, but Star didn't think she'd be using it much because, although she enjoyed cooking, she did enough of it at the café.

The small box that held her mother's crystal collection was in the box of precious things, and she lined the colorful stones up on the windowsill over the kitchen table: Purple amethyst, yellow citrine, a chunk of turquoise they'd found together in the desert when Star was ten. A dozen in all. Her mother, Poppy, had ascribed magical and medicinal properties to each, but Star just liked the way they caught the light, and how they reminded her of her mom.

Next, she carefully unpacked the handmade glass vase she'd found in a thrift store in Utah. She knew a bit about glass from a short stint working with some glass blowers in Colorado, and this piece, with the blue and green swirls and punty marks on the bottom where the artisans had broken it off the blow pipe, was a real find. She liked to fill it with colorful flowers, wildflowers in summer and, her one extravagance, grocery store blooms in the winter months.

She set the vase on a small side table at the foot of the attic stairs. Above it, china ladies danced their way across a shelf and on the wall beside them, the black and white photograph of Augusta. Star took a moment to study it more carefully. Augusta's face at the car window had an exuberant smile, as if life was an open road ahead, there for the taking.

Star could relate to that feeling. After the shock of her mother's death had worn off, that was how she had felt when she decided to take Eden, her only real inheritance, and hit the road. Off on a grand adventure. What her mother would have wanted.

Now, three years later, that grand adventure was a wee bit tarnished. She wasn't sure what she'd thought she would find out there, and although she'd met many interesting people and done lots of, well, mostly boring jobs, something vital was missing in her life. She wasn't sure what. Job satisfaction? That was for sure. She was determined to spend the winter looking for something she could sink her teeth into. Something more fulfilling than slinging burgers.

A new life and someone to share it with?

Now where had *that* idea come from? She frowned at the

photograph on the wall, remembering what Lily had said about Augusta being something of a matchmaker.

She shook her head and turned away from the photograph. No. Getting tied down with a man was the last thing she needed. Who knew when she might want to hit the road? Although it would be nice to go out on a date occasionally, she didn't need the complications that always ensued. From observing her mother's life, she knew you couldn't count on a man to stick around. Her father hadn't stayed, and none of the men her mother had tangled up with over the years had been with them for more than a few months. Then her mother, always the fragile Blanche Dubois, would be devastated, and they'd hit the road again. Until the next town and the next man.

And where were these men when you needed them? Where had they been when her mother got sick and it had been up to Star to keep a roof over their heads and care for her while she wasted away?

No, she'd decided long ago she was better off on her own, and she'd pretty well given up looking. But that didn't mean she didn't enjoy a bit of male companionship every once in a while. Sometimes it was lonely, living alone. If she was going to spend the winter in Fortune Bay, could be nice to have a warm body to cuddle with under the sheets.

"Okay, Augusta," she said aloud to the empty room. "Let's see what you've got."

Chapter 3

❄ ❄ ❄ ❄ ❄ ❄

A nasty wind blew in off the lake, pushing Star down the drive as she started out to Lily's for dinner. Luckily, the farmhouse Marshall and Lily had just moved into was right across the road.

Darkness came early at this time of year, and although Star had left the porch light on at the cabin, she fished a small flashlight out of her shoulder bag as she headed up the lane, and trained it on the ground. Potholes and rocks under the thin layer of snow could twist an ankle faster than you could say *hare krishna.*

A clot of wet snow slid off an overhead branch and splatted on her head, icy water dribbling down her back. She wound her chunky knit scarf more tightly around her neck. Even with the heavy sweater underneath, her jean jacket was not nearly warm enough for this damp weather. But, when you're five foot one and a half inches tall, it's not easy to find adult clothing that fits. And considering that, because of her size, people already tended to treat her as much younger than her thirty-three years, wearing brightly colored children's slickers didn't help. If she was going to spend another winter in Fortune Bay, it was time to find an adult upgrade to her apparel. There wasn't much available in her size in the second-hand store in Majestic, so she might have to go farther afield to find a women's jacket that fit.

The overcast sky blocked out the moon, and although the main road was not much brighter than the lane had been, at least it had been plowed so there wasn't the threat of hidden potholes. The farm driveway was only a couple of hundred feet down the road on the opposite side, and soon

Star was crunching up the gravel driveway towards the beckoning light on the farmhouse porch.

The farm belonged to Stephanie Murphy, who also owned the cabin. Stephanie had inherited the old log farmhouse from her late husband's family and often rented it out, this time to Lily, Marshall and his kids. The first house to be built in the area, Star was familiar with the black and white photographs that hung in the café of oxen skidding the giant logs along snow roads to the building site over one hundred years ago.

Tonight, lights burned in every window illuminating the smoke that puffed from the chimney, all combining to give the old building a cheerful, lived-in air. Until last week, Lily's father Max had lived there alone, but in a major shuffle of living arrangements in the community last weekend, Max had moved in with his girlfriend Stephanie, and Marshall and Lily moved into the log house leaving the cabin free for Star.

She had never been inside the farmhouse before, so when she reached the front door, she knocked.

It swung open immediately and a tall man's broad shoulders filled the bright rectangle. Harry Brewster was the kind of man who always both attracted and scared her. Not by any threat of violence—Harry was always extremely polite and self-contained—but by the inexplicable way her legs seemed to melt in the presence of his quiet strength.

Emily, Lily's six-year-old step-daughter, darted in front of him. "I've been waiting for you *forever.*"

"Well, I'm here now," Star answered, her voice muffled by the woolly scarf that covered the lower half of her face.

Harry stepped aside so she could enter. Pulling off her sopping wet knit cap, she shook it out the door, drops of melting snow flying in every direction. Then she handed it to Harry and unwound the striped knit scarf, quickly running her fingers through the red curls she was sure now suffered from a severe case of hat-head.

"Terrible weather," he said. "Let me take your coat."

"Thank you." Harry was always flawlessly polite, and Star never had a clue what he was thinking. With a shy smile, she relinquished her jean jacket, which was also soaking wet, then turned to Emily. "How do you like your new house?"

"It's not a *new* house," Emily said, her almost-black eyes serious. "It's a very *old* house. It has a furnace made of wood."

"No, dummy," Boz interrupted, chest pumped out, eager to impress. "It burns wood, not made of wood. It's made of, you know, furnace stuff."

"Cast iron," Harry said. Star looked up to find him watching her, but then he turned abruptly away and hung her wet clothes on the coat rack in the hall. "Come and sit by the fire. You look a little blue."

"The wind is raw off the water tonight."

"You walked?"

"She lives across the road now," Boz said, perching on the arm of Harry's chair. "You dummy."

"Don't 'you dummy' me." Harry grabbed Boz in a headlock and gave his hair a brisk knuckle rub. Boz laughed in feigned terror and wrestled his way out of the hold but, Star noticed, he didn't leave his perch.

"Lily should be down in a moment," Harry said.

Silence bloomed in the warm room. Usually Star could fill any void in the conversation, but with Harry she never knew what to say. They were from different worlds, his all business and first-class travel, and hers all makeshift and make-do. She chewed on her lip. His expression was shuttered. Either he was bored or, what? Shy? Doubtful. He'd been on the road touring Marshall's country rock band for twenty years and must have been with a lot of women. He couldn't be shy.

But he made her uncomfortable, like other powerful

men in her past: bosses she'd had and, as a girl, the popular local guys who seemed to rule the school halls. To break the silence, she asked, "So, are you staying here with Marshall and Lily?"

His deep laugh surprised her and, thankfully, she felt the tension lessen. "I couldn't impose. The four of them barely fit in this house as it is. I'm staying in Marshall's old cottage at the resort in Fortune Bay."

"Just a visit?"

He frowned. "I'm helping him look for a place to open a recording studio."

"Here?"

"Maybe here." His frown deepened, and he leaned forward, forearms resting on his thighs, and looked at the floor. "The problem is...I'm not sure I'm ready to relocate."

Then he looked up as if surprised he'd said that out loud, shook his head and gave a slightly embarrassed laugh. "But we'll see. Please don't mention that last part to Marshall."

"I won't," Lily said, appearing in the doorway. "But you two better figure that out. And soon."

"We will." Harry said firmly.

Lily retreated from the doorway. "Come into the kitchen."

Emily held her tiny hand out to Star. "I'll show you the way."

Taking Emily's fingers, Star let her lead the way, but a prickle ran down the back of her neck at the awareness that Harry followed behind.

"Are you still working at the ice cream store?" Emily asked, the awe on her face saying more than words could express just how great she thought a job scooping ice cream would be.

"You sell ice cream?" Harry asked, leaning against the doorframe.

"I'm the cook at the café in the general store," Star said,

taking a seat at the kitchen table. "In the summer we sell old fashioned ice cream cones. Marshall and Lily often brought the kids in."

"I've only been in the store once, when I set up Marshall's meal account," Harry said.

"I know." Star had been uncomfortably aware whenever Harry had been visiting ever since they'd met last summer at Marshall's cottage at the resort, and she would have known if he'd come into the store. Sometimes Lily had taken her to the cottage for a swim after work, and sometimes Harry had been there. Once it had turned into dinner followed by a raging game of Yahtzee. She'd been surprised how relaxed Harry had been with the children considering how stiff and polite he always was with her. He remained an enigma, his reserve with her only intensifying her discomfort.

He walked over to the stove, lifted the lid of a big pot and a delicious aroma swirled into the room.

Star's mouth began to water, and she realized how hungry she was. "That smells amazing."

"Dinner's all Harry and Marshall tonight," Lily said, slipping two frozen pies into the oven.

"You cook?" Star asked, turning those hypnotic amber eyes on Harry and, once again, his mind went blank. He never knew what to say to her. She was ethereal, like a fairy, not quite of this world. A smile quirked his lips at the irony. He met beautiful women in L.A. every day—hell, he'd even met movie stars—but none of them made him squirm the way Star did.

"A bit," he said. "It's just stew. But it's been cooking all day, so it's got that layered aroma." *Layered aroma?* What was he, hosting a cable cooking show? He cleared his throat. "I'm trying to teach Marshall some life skills."

"Hey, I've got skills." Marshall Mason walked casually

into the room. Despite the angry patch of recently grafted skin that ran over one cheek from his eye to his jaw and the bandage that still covered his hand, Harry had to admit he'd never seen his old friend look so relaxed and happy. Harry hadn't realized how much pressure Marshall had been under for the past ten—no, make that twenty—years. Not until Marsh had emerged from the trauma of last year's motorcycle accident, with Lily at his side. But surely this small-town, I-want-to-stay-in-Fortune-Bay stage was temporary. Marshall couldn't be serious about relocating to this backwater town.

Sure, it was nice for a day or two in the summer, like when Marshall and the kids had been staying at the resort in town. But to stay here all winter? What was the point? Hadn't they gotten enough of winter as kids in Minnesota? Harry sure had.

Lily gave Marshall a saucy look. "Harry has a point. You'll have to pick up the slack while I'm at work until your housekeeper gets up here to give you a hand." She turned to Harry. "Did you find any interesting houses on the lake online?"

"I did not." And he wasn't going to knock himself out trying because, sooner or later, Marshall would come to his senses and come back to the City of Angels.

Marshall Mason had been a multi-platinum award winning country singer. A star. But now that he couldn't perform anymore, he and Harry were talking about starting a new business together, a recording studio. But not here. Not in Fortune Bay.

They'd been together since their high school garage band days, when Harry had briefly tried to play the drums but had quickly realized he couldn't carry a tune or hold a beat to save his soul. He did have an ear though, and right from the start he'd been Marshall's biggest fan and staunchest ally. He was the one to find the band their first gigs: birthdays, and later, school dances, where Marshall in particular had been a big swoon.

When they were eighteen, they'd moved to Nashville. They had struggled to make enough money to eat, so Harry had asked around and found the names of the bars and honky-tonks across the country where the other guys started out and put together their first tour. Six months on the road with six stinky guys in a van, a different venue every night, different women—for the band at least—in every town. Then they did it all over again. And again, and again, working their way up through the circuit until they were opening for big country names like Brad Paisley and Reba McEntire. Then finally, they were the main act.

Marshall had never able to keep his shit together—not that he did drugs or drank excessively. His head was just always in the music, and if he hadn't been so darn talented, Harry didn't know what would have become of him.

So Harry had taken care of everything. He loved the planning, if not always the day to day scrimping and driving and finding the next greasy spoon for dinner. He had pushed and planned until now they could eat in the best restaurants anywhere in the world. And where were they? Friggin' Fortune Bay.

Sooner or later Marsh had to see that this plan of his, of theirs, to produce, would work better in L.A., or, if need be, Nashville.

"The look on your face when you found out the kids were descending on you for the summer!" Lily mimicked his terrified voice. "'What will I feed them? What do children eat?'"

"Ice cream," Emily shouted gleefully.

"We got by," Marshall said good naturedly in his own defense.

Lily looked scornful. "Only because you had Star at the café and then the hotel chef feeding you and your hungry brood."

Suddenly it twigged. When Harry had moved Marsh into the cottage at the resort after his surgery, the resort kitchen hadn't even been open yet, so he'd set up that food plan for Marshall with the owner of the general store and café. He hadn't realized until that moment, that was where Star worked.

He looked at Star. "The café."

She raised her chin. "For now."

He shook his head. So here they were, back to eating in greasy spoons. "Yes, so I'm trying to teach his nibs a few of the basics of feeding a family. Stew, stir fry, hamburgers."

Star turned to Marshall in amazement. "Hamburgers? You don't know how to make hamburgers?"

Marshall held up his hands helplessly. "We were on the road forty weeks a year. When would I learn to cook?" Then a sweet smile crossed his still slightly crooked lips. He put an arm around Lily and kissed her temple. "I'm looking forward to spending my days at home from now on. I just need you, Harry, to find one for us."

And so it had always been. And Harry had always come through for Marsh, so why should Marshall expect that to change?

But Harry was ready to start a new chapter in his life, too. A new bend in his career path, maybe find a place to settle down. He just couldn't see doing that in Fortune Bay.

Chapter 4
❄ ❄ ❄ ❄ ❄ ❄

Star sprayed the industrial cleaner on the stainless stove top and wiped off the worst of the spattered grease with a heavy-duty paper towel. If she never cooked another burger, she'd think she'd died and gone to heaven. She tried, but she knew from the reaction of the customers that her burgers weren't even very good. Too many were left for garbage on the plate. She was surprised Fiona kept her on as the short-order cook here. She had to find a new gig.

She sprayed the prep surface and wiped it down, taking advantage of this quiet moment after the noon rush to get the place back in shape. As she scrubbed off the burger spatter, her thoughts went to Harry, again, and her lips turned up in a smile. She hadn't been able to think about anything else since dinner last night. He was dynamic and cool, so different from the other men she'd met while drifting around the west for most of her life. He had a sheen of confidence and determination that set him apart. But she'd seen a soft side, too, how easy he was with the children. He was someone you could count on.

She resumed scrubbing with renewed vigor. She couldn't get hung-up on a man now. Especially not a man who, from what he'd said last night, wasn't planning on staying in Fortune Bay. And what was she thinking? Neither was she.

But she'd been so physically aware of him, she'd hardly been able to carry on a conversation. The way his shirt fit tight across his broad shoulders and chest, as if his clothes had been made for him. But great as that looked, she sensed tension in the body beneath those clothes. She wanted to get him into jeans and a flannel shirt and muss up his hair.

There were creative ways beyond yoga to get that hard body to relax.

When she looked up from the greasy counter, there he was. *Ohmygod.* Walking into the café. A hot flush crashed over her like a tidal wave. He strode in like a man used to being in charge, stopping just inside the arched doorway like he was checking out the place for a meal for the crew. Lily had said that had been part of his job when they were on the road, keeping the band and roadies fed and housed and out of trouble.

Star wondered what his job was now.

Okay, so he was in jeans today, but they had been pressed—*seriously?*—and fit his hips and legs like a glove. His brown leather jacket looked as if it had been tailored by Armani. If Armani made leather jackets. She had no idea.

Praying he couldn't tell she'd been thinking about him, she tried to flash a casual smile. "So, you found us."

The smile he returned was smooth. "I did. I thought I'd get away from the rowdy crowd at the farm and try a cup of your famous coffee."

Now she had a real reason to smile. "I do make good coffee. And how about a sticky bun?"

He hesitated.

"Don't worry. I didn't make them."

His brows drew together. "I didn't mean—"

She waved a hand. "No offense taken. It's a well-known fact that while my coffee rocks, my baking is usually, well, rocks."

He laughed, the sound so genuine that she started to relax. "Louise made them," she continued, picking up a sticky bun with tongs, putting it on a plate and setting it before him. "She's the best pastry chef in the valley."

Harry settled on one of the red vinyl stools at the counter and picked up the bun. Sugary frosting oozed down the side and over his fingers and he licked it off like a kid. Then he took a big bite and groaned. "Curse you, Starlight Angel, for introducing me to these wickedly delicious treats."

"That's me," she said, flashing him a smile. "Starlight—although I'm rarely called an angel."

He stopped before the next bite. "Starlight? Seriously?"

She shrugged helplessly. "What can I say? My mom was a bona fide hippy."

He looked up at her from under crazy-thick black lashes, and his voice dropped. "Was?"

His chocolate brown eyes, fixed intently on her, conveyed a depth of concern she found difficult to handle. So, she shrugged. "She died. Three years ago."

"I'm so sorry." The softening of his expression was almost her undoing, the timbre of his voice striking a chord that had tears forming in her eyes.

She blinked, grabbed a wet rag and started mopping the counter. "Well, it is what it is." Then she said brightly, "How's that coffee? Can I top it up?"

He smiled. "Excellent coffee." And he held out his empty mug for a refill.

As she poured him a fresh cup, she remembered her news. "I wanted to tell you. I asked around this morning and got a few leads on places that might work for you guys."

He frowned. "Who guys?"

"You know, what you and Marshall were talking about last night. A house with room for a studio. I didn't quite understand, though. What exactly are you planning to do?"

"We're starting a production company. Marshall's still writing and, who knows, he might get his voice back, although his hand will never be dexterous enough to play the guitar professionally again. But he's an amazing writer and arranger, and other artists are eager to record his songs. We can't do it here though."

Star leaned back against the prep counter and fisted one hand under her chin. "Why not?"

Harry looked at her like she was crazy. "In Fortune Bay?"

"Why not? If you had a studio, with Marshall's name and your obvious connections I don't see why it wouldn't be a success."

"There's more to it than that," Harry blustered.

Star smiled at him, nonplussed. "Like what?"

"Well, like transportation, accommodation, an infrastructure."

"We've got that here. Float planes land here all the time. And there's the resort for accommodation and food and— what do you mean, 'infrastructure'?"

"The industry. People to call on, I don't know, the scene."

"Do you really need the scene to produce an album?"

"Of course you do," he said indignantly, as if caught in a lie—or an exaggeration.

An uncomfortable silence followed. Maybe she'd pushed too hard. She wiped the already clean counter again and glanced up at him.

Harry took a quick sip of his coffee and shot her a look. "So, you're quite a Fortune Bay booster," he said, holding her gaze. "For someone who's not hanging around."

Her smile faltered. That was true. She wasn't going to stay. There was nothing for her here, except some new friends, but she could find friends anywhere. Well, maybe not like these friends, but, new friends. And she certainly wouldn't stay for the job. Unless something better turned up pretty darn quick, she'd be out of here, on to the next town. Yes sir-ee.

y z T

She had him bewitched. There was no other explanation for how she had talked Harry into going to look at those places she'd lined up.

He was back at the farm, killing an hour before he was to pick her up outside the General Store after her shift. Marshall had been thrilled by his progress on the project but when Harry suggested Marsh come along, he'd said Harry should do the preliminary search himself. That the studio had been his idea. That all Marshall was looking for was a big old farmhouse on the lake to settle down in with his family. Anyway, he'd argued, he had to stay and wait for the kids to get home from school since Lily was still at work at the resort.

The kids were an iron-clad excuse, but Harry thought Marshall probably just wanted to work on his current song-in-progress. He sighed. And that was okay, because writing hit songs that other artists wanted to record was a crucial part of their new business plan. The footwork had always been Harry's job.

Normally he didn't mind, enjoyed the planning and the hunt for new venues, *but they weren't staying in Fortune Bay.* So that made this hunt a waste of time.

Yet here he was, climbing into the car and heading back to the village to pick up Star to go and look at houses. He'd met hundreds of women over the years, and dated a few, but he was usually the go-to guy, the guy who got things done, not the one who wined and dined the ladies. Or, in the early days, the one who took them out for burgers and beer in the honky-tonks.

In many ways, he missed those days. It was the wild west of gigging and recording. Every night a new adventure. Would the van break down? He was always the one to crawl under and fix it since he was the only one with an ounce of mechanical sense. Would the acoustics in the hall—or lack thereof—demand constant fine-tuning of the sound board so the words and music weren't just a mash of ear-splitting noise? That was his job, too, in the early days, before Stan-the-sound-guy joined the team. He'd enjoyed working the soundboard. It made him feel like he was contributing, like he was part of the band. And he thought he had an ear for it, too. Marshall had always said he did, but eventually the entourage got too big and the arrangements became too complicated, and he'd had to let that part of the job go. Kind of a shame.

Then came the accident and Marshall dropped off the map—or seemed to, to the outside world—and Harry's job had changed from being Marshall's right-hand man to taking care of him in other ways. He'd sat by his hospital bed for weeks when Marsh's ex-wife couldn't be bothered and wouldn't let the kids visit. He'd fought off the paparazzi when Marshall got out of the hospital. And had found him a retreat deep in the woods at the Majestic Resort in which to recover. It hadn't been open to the public yet but Max Finster, the manager, Lily's dad, had agreed to rent a cottage for a price they were willing to pay for peace and anonymity.

During the past year, Harry had tried to fill in for Marshall; getting the last album out, handling the ensuing publicity and finally, receiving the CMA award for the album. At the same time, he'd set up Marshall's extended surgeries, basically waiting for the other shoe to drop and for Marshall to come back to his old life in L.A.

And he got it, he really did. Marshall's old life was not coming back. His performing career was over, but with their connections in the music industry they could move on to phase two. Whatever that turned out to be.

And it had already begun, despite Marshall dragging his feet. He'd written a song—to Lily, Harry suspected—and a young up-and-comer Harry had discovered in a Burbank coffee house had recorded it. When the song had gone on to be a substantial hit, Harry had thought, this is it. This will show Marsh that there's life after the accident.

But what does Marsh do? He moves to the friggin' middle of nowhere. Friggin' Fortune Bay.

Chapter 5
❋ ❋ ❋ ❋ ❋ ❋

When Harry pulled the rented, black, Mercedes SUV into the parking lot of the General Store, he immediately spotted Star, a waif wrapped in layers of denim and multi-colored knit pieces that he'd be at a loss to describe, huddled on the cold cement front step.

He reached across the seat and threw open the door. "Climb in. You look frozen. Why didn't you wait inside?" As she clambered in, he held out a hand and helped her up onto the seat.

"I wanted some fresh air. I needed to get away from the smell of coffee and French fries."

Once she was settled, she smiled across the big seat at him and his spirits rebounded. Maybe this wouldn't be so bad. The late afternoon sun was shining and suddenly he was looking forward to an hour's drive with a pretty lady through the picturesque valley between the mountains, looking at houses he was sure were not going to be what they were looking for but, hey, who cares, if it meant he got to spend an hour with Star.

The tires ground on the loose gravel as he pulled out of the lot. "Where to?"

Star pulled a scrap of paper out of the fringed bag she had tucked between the colorful layers of the woolly poncho she wore over her jean jacket. Her fingers were slightly blue, but she just blew on them, gave them a quick flex, then looked at the paper. "The first place is about five miles down the road, on this side of Majestic, but the other two places are around the other side of the lake on this road. It's really the only road. It goes halfway around the lake."

As they drove through village, snow-capped mountains formed a jagged horizon across the dark water. "What comes after that?"

"The rest of the lake is in the National Park and the National Forest." She sat on the edge of her seat like a child. "This is fun. My van's been out of commission since I got here so I don't get out of Fortune Bay very often. I've had to count on friends to even get to Majestic. Or take the bus. I haven't been to Seattle since I got here."

"How long ago was that?" Harry asked as the big car cruised out of the town and back into the forest.

"A year." She stopped for a minute, then shook her head in amazement. "I've never lived anywhere that long in my life."

"Really?" He was silent for a moment. "I guess I've been on the road my whole adult life, too. Too busy to settle down."

"Did you want to? Settle down?"

"Not really. Never saw the point. There was always so much to see and do. It kind of seemed like, I don't know, settling. For second best."

She nodded. "Right. I've pretty much been on the road my whole life. It's all I know."

"Even through your childhood?"

She nodded. "Yup. It was always just my mom and me."

"No father?"

She pressed her lips together and shook her head.

"No grandparents?"

Her eyes widened as if that was an important subject. "No. I always wanted grandparents, though."

A vision of holiday dinners with his unruly family, brothers, sisters, two sets of grandparents, flashed through his mind. "So, just you and your mom."

"Mm-hmm. We travelled a lot, never stayed in one place for very long so I never made very many friends."

"You must have had friends at school."

"Not so much. I was home schooled part of the time, and other times we were in and out of one town after another. My mom said it kept things fresh but, looking back, I think she just couldn't settle. I guess I learned that from her."

Harry thought about how long he and Marshall had been friends. How their friendship had changed their lives. How important it was to him still. Star hadn't had that.

She was silent for a moment, then said, "My childhood was...unconventional." She nodded as if that was a word she could live with. "My mother was a free spirit."

Harry smiled, but kept his eyes on the winding road. "You must take after her."

Star drew a horrified breath. "Not at all. She couldn't keep a job or a roof over our heads for more than a few months at a time." She stopped, pressed her lips together and gave a sad smile. "She did her best, but I'm not at all like her. I leave because I want to. It's always my decision."

"But you always leave."

"Well, yes." She looked out the window to the afternoon sun filtering through the towering Douglas Firs. "So far."

"Sounds like you're thinking of changing that. Maybe staying here?"

She sighed. "I think I might like to, but I don't think I can. The people are so nice and welcoming. I've never really fit in anywhere else before." She turned to him and said earnestly, "But I think I could, here." Then she faced the road, settling back in her seat with a sigh. "But I don't want to work at the café much longer. I'd like to find something I enjoy doing. I'm not sure what that is yet, but there aren't many opportunities in Fortune Bay."

"I know what you mean."

They drove in silence for a few minutes until they came to an S-curve in the road. "We're here. Mr. Milne, the owner of this property, said the driveway should be right here, on the left."

They turned down a rutted lane but instead of driving down to the lake, it curled up a steep hillside. Halfway to the top, the road ended at a small cabin made of rough boards, something that could at one time have been a fishing shack or hunt camp.

Harry stopped the car and they surveyed the shack. From the look of it, no one had lived there for many years. And no one would want to.

"I guess the property goes over the hill and down to the lake," Star said doubtfully.

Harry shook his head and put the car in reverse. "We don't want to build from scratch. Marsh wants something he can move the family into quickly. They're finding the farm too small already." He made a two-point turn in a small clearing, drove back to the main road and stopped. "Next?"

"Turn left. The two other places are past Majestic, around the other side of the lake."

It didn't take long to get to Majestic—and even less time to drive through the town. "I don't know why Marshall wants to stay here," Harry muttered as he waited for a string of day-care children to straggle across the road.

"Well, I'd imagine Lily is a big factor. I guess your girlfriend wouldn't go for it?"

His lips quirked in a smile—she was fishing—but he kept his eyes on the road. "No girlfriend." Out of the corner of his eye, he thought he saw her lips press together in a smug smile. He darted her a side glance. "And you?"

She looked out the side window. "Nope. No one."

Of course not. It sounded like she never stayed in one place long enough to form a serious relationship.

"The next place is just a couple of miles down the road," she said. "Both places in fact. They're side-by-side."

This side of the lake was even more remote than Fortune Bay. No cute little town or houses in sight, just a few driveways snaking off through the trees, and a faded sign that read, '*Porter's Marina, 6 miles.*'

"There it is." Star pointed to a hand-painted sign that said *Tariton*, nailed to a tree. Harry turned the SUV toward the lake and they bounced down the drive.

At the end of the road, they stopped in a clearing where low, angled sunlight lit up the wet lawn, surrounding trees and overgrown garden, making it glitter like a fairyland.

The house was quaint, at least fifty years old, two story with dormers looking out to the lake over a wide porch. The shake siding was natural cedar, but the trim was painted yellow and white, giving the place a storybook quality.

"I love it," Star breathed.

Cute, but— "Too small," Harry declared.

Star climbed out of the car while it was still running. "Let's go in anyway. I have a key."

Harry turned off the ignition and reluctantly followed her up onto the porch. "I guess we can look, but Marshall wants something bigger. He said at least four bedrooms and three baths."

Star wasn't listening. She just put the key in the lock and swung open the door. The house had been built with care, with wide baseboards and a gleaming expanse of wood floors throughout the living and dining rooms. A picture window faced the lake, and as she stood before it and took in the view, she folded her hands at her chest and drew a deep breath. Then she sent him an excited smile that melted his heart and rushed through the door at the end of the short hall by the stairs, into a large kitchen.

"A real family kitchen," she said reverently, her fingers tracing the lines on the door frame where each child had been measured, year after year. "Full of memories." She sighed. "I can almost hear people laughing and dishes clinking."

Harry looked around. To him it was just a typical family

kitchen, kind of out of date, like the kitchen of his childhood and that of a million other kids. But Star's face was rapturous. He couldn't look away.

She turned and seemed almost surprised to find him still there. Her cheeks turned pink and she laughed. "You must think I'm crazy, but as a child I always wanted a home like this." Then, eyes bright with excitement, she added, "Let's check upstairs." And raced out of the room.

Harry followed in her wake. A thousand hands had burnished the oak newel post and bannister to a soft glow. "Well built," he allowed as he followed her up the stairs.

"These rooms are so cute," Star called from one of the back bedrooms.

Harry ducked through the low doorway to join her in a small bedroom with a sloped ceiling. "A little small."

Star ran her hand over the faded wallpaper. "A child's room. I always wanted a room like this when I was little."

In the bathroom, a deep porcelain tub with claw feet stood on a floor of white hexagonal porcelain tiles that continued halfway up the walls.

Star was one step ahead of him, and Harry followed her into the front master bedroom, decorated with soft, flowery wallpaper and more glowing wood floors.

She was sitting on a window seat built into one of the dormer windows over the porch, the sunlight streaming in from behind lighting her hair in a halo of fire. Her eyes were big and bright. "I'd want a soft carpet and a big poster bed." She laughed and shook her head. "Sorry. Just dreaming."

He smiled at her excitement but didn't say anything, just looked around, trying to see the room through her eyes. Yes, he could see her on a big, four poster bed.

The house reminded him of his grandparents' home in Minnesota, and while it wasn't what they were looking for today, Star obviously loved it.

"I could never afford a place like this," she said wistfully.

"It's nice, but not big enough."

"For you or for Marshall?"

He looked at her in surprise. "For Marshall. I'm not looking for a place for myself."

"Would you live with them?"

He was confused. "No, but I don't really think we're moving here at all."

"Humph," she *humphed*, getting up off the window seat and heading for the door. "I think, if you looked, you would see that Marshall already has."

He frowned at her words but didn't comment as he followed her back to the car.

The third property was right next door, but that entailed driving down the long driveway through the trees, one hundred feet further along the main road, then back toward the lake on an even longer drive. Halfway down the lane, Harry slowed the car as they passed a large, new, two-story garage, or maybe a workshop, then drove on to stop in front of a large house. It sat on a point of land that jutted out into the lake giving it a one-hundred-and-eighty-degree view of the water. Extensive grounds and gardens had paths that led down to a small sandy beach next to a dock and boathouse.

Shit. It was perfect.

"This belongs to Jules Tariton, too," Star said. "His uncle lived here and bought the house next door for his mother. When they both died, Jules inherited both places."

She poked around the yard but, strangely, didn't seem nearly as impressed with this more lavish property as she had been with the smaller house next door. But still she said, "This would be perfect for Marshall and Lily. We should tell them right away. Waterfront goes quickly."

She was right. It ticked all of Marshall's boxes. Size, location, even a perfect studio right on the property.

"I guess we have to tell them." Harry forced a smile. "Marshall will be pleased."

Half an hour later he pulled the SUV up to the cabin to drop Star off. Suddenly, he felt like the awkward, tubby fifteen-year-old boy he had been in high school. "Come for dinner tomorrow night? At my cottage at the resort?" Why did he always sound so stiff when he spoke to this woman? *Dummy.* It was obvious—he cared what she thought of him.

Star smiled. "I'd love to. Shall I just walk over after work? Six o'clock?"

He let out a pent-up breath. "Perfect."

Chapter 6
✻ ✻ ✻ ❁ ✻ ✻

The next day, after her shift, Star ducked into the tiny washroom at the café with the over-sized shoulder bag she'd brought with her that morning, and studied her reflection in the mirror, checking the damage an eight-hour shift had wrought. It hadn't made sense to go all the way back to the cabin between work and dinner since Harry's cottage at the resort was basically across the road, so she had planned her strategy like a campaign.

She had gotten up early—before dawn—to wash her hair and had twisted it into a knot on top of her head. Now, when she pulled out the clasps, it fell in gentle curls to her shoulders. *Success!* Not always a sure thing. Then she tugged off the grease spattered tunic she'd worn all day over her leggings, pulled a diaphanous green and gold top from her bag, her go-to sexy outfit, and shook it out. A miracle fabric, the wrinkles fell away, and she pulled it over her head. As she turned this way and that in front of the small mirror, she was pleased to see that the soft fabric clung to her breasts, showing off what little she had to the best advantage.

She used a paper towel to wipe the sheen left from working over the hot stove all day off her face and, cursing the dim light, applied some smoky eye makeup. Looking more closely, she wiped a smudge off her cheek and hoped it was the only one. Then she pulled out a sample bottle of perfume, a light scent that smelled of roses, and spritzed it into the air, letting it fall over her lightly like a spring shower.

Then she stuffed everything back in her bag and was ready to go.

It was just dinner, she told herself as she pulled on her

jean jacket and wound her scarf around her neck, careful not to disturb her hair. Lily and Marshall would probably be there. And maybe the kids. They were getting to be a "thing', a group, a gang. She liked the feeling of family that was developing with these casual, last minute dinner invitations. She'd rarely had a group of friends like this, and it was exciting.

Waving goodbye to Fiona as she walked through the store, she stepped outside into the darkness and was hit by a bitter wind. As soon as snow covered the surrounding mountaintops, the air temperature around the lake chilled, whether they had snow at the lower elevation or not. Luckily, today was not, and the ground was dry under her turquoise cowboy boots. They weren't the best choice for the generally-wet Fortune Bay weather, but they were the best she had.

She wrapped her scarf more tightly around her chin and looked up to the heavens where stars spangled the sky, as good a show as anything her mother had ever made with her bedazzler. That was one legacy of Poppy's that Star had been happy to leave behind. Her clothing may still not be mainstream, at least she no longer sparkled when she walked. Most of the time. She still had a few pieces in her closet that she pulled out for special occasions.

The entrance to the resort was directly across the road, Blue's big sign with carved eagles flying over the lake pointing the way. Lights dotted the paved road that wound through the trees to the parking lot and the main pavilion. She cut across the parking lot to a path that led through a bit of light bush and across the point to the cottages along the far shore. A few moments later, she was walking up to Harry's front porch.

It was surprisingly quiet. She'd expected to hear chatting voices through the door. She must be the first one there. Her stomach flipped at the thought of being alone with

Harry, of having to make conversation until the others arrived.

Don't be silly. You were alone with him in the car for an hour yesterday and that went well.

Putting a smile on her face, she took a deep breath and knocked.

y z T

When he heard the knock on the door, Harry's eyes darted around the small kitchen. The tiny table was set, complete with candles. Kitchen wasn't too much of a mess. He was ready. Turning down the heat under the Beef Bourguignon, he dimmed the kitchen lights and went to the door. With his hand on the knob, he whipped off the dishtowel-apron he'd forgotten he'd tied around his waist and hung it on a coat hook. Then he paused for a moment to take a breath. *Get a grip.*

He had an apartment in L.A., but he'd been on the road most of the time so he rarely entertained. And never a woman, alone, for dinner. The cottage was perfect for that, though, with a nice living room complete with soft couches and a cozy gas fireplace, separate bedrooms and a well-stocked kitchen. With the lights low, it was an intimate setting for a date. It had worked for Marshall. Who knows? It might work for him, too.

He threw open the door and his heart stumbled when he saw her. Bundled up as usual. He just wanted to unwind that scarf...

"Hi," she said, tilting her head questioningly.

He shook off his daze and stepped aside. "Hello. Come right in."

She stepped inside. "I see I'm the first one here," she said brightly as she unwound her scarf and shrugged out of her jacket.

He felt like an idiot. She didn't know it was a date. He

should have been clearer. "You're the only one. No one else is coming."

Her eyebrows raised, hopefully not in alarm. Then she smiled. "Smells delicious." Following her nose to the kitchen, she put her hand on the lid of the pot on the stove and turned her pixy grin on him. "May I?"

"Of course. Hungry?"

"I am. Even though I work with food all day, I don't usually eat. After a while the smell of French-fries and burgers gets kind of nauseating."

"Well then, let's get this show on the road." He turned on the burner under the pot for the noodles and slipped the vegetables into the oven for roasting, glad he had everything ready. "Working at the diner's not your thing?"

"Not at all," she said, with an exaggerated shudder. Then she smiled. "I like the people, but I could do without the cooking." She slipped onto one of the stools at the kitchen counter. "It's mostly the menu there that I object to. I actually like cooking. Just never had much of a chance. I'd like to cook for a big family. You know, if I had one."

What could he say to that? "Wine?"

Her sad smile perked up. "Sure."

He'd used most of the bottle of Burgundy for the beef, so he opened another and handed her a glass. "This won't take long."

"So, what did Marshall say about the house? He must have been happy."

"He was, but I still don't know if it's a good idea."

Star raised her brows and looked at him over the rim of her wineglass. "Isn't it up to him and Lily?"

"It is, but we were going to be partners in the studio, so that kind of makes it a joint decision. I just can't see us setting it up here for the long term."

She looked at him, her amber cat's eyes hypnotic under a cloud of fiery curls. "Maybe you just need more of a reason to stay."

Maybe, if she were a permanent fixture in his life, he might grow to like this quirky town.

Chapter 7

❄ ❄ ❄ ❄ ❄ ❄

His deep brown eyes, warm and gooey as melting chocolate, stared deep into the depth of her soul as he swept her into his arms. Whoa! That must be the wine talking. Star had barely had a sip but was feeling much more relaxed than when she'd arrived. Good food, excellent wine, a handsome—no *gorgeous*—guy, who normally she would have considered way out of her league, but who seemed quite happy to talk to her. Her dream date, really, because this, she was beginning to realize, was what it was. A date. With Harry. Really.

He'd lit *candles* on the table and had prepared a fancy meal cooked in wine. So far from the burgers she was slinging, she could hardly adjust. It was heaven.

When they finished the main course, he said, "Let's take our desert into the living room."

That sounded wonderful, sitting together on the couch... "More wine?"

Hell, yes. She wasn't driving. She held out her glass.

Desert was a confection of chocolate and cream in puffy pastry. "Louise?" she asked after the first luscious mouthful.

He nodded. "I ordered it from the resort kitchen."

"Good choice."

They made short work of the pastry, then Harry topped up her glass and took their plates to the kitchen. Sighing in contentment, Star leaned back on the couch and stared into the leaping flames in the fireplace.

Harry came back from the kitchen and this time took a seat on the couch beside her. The food and wine had done their job and she wanted nothing more than to snuggle up beside this big, cozy, bear of a man, so when he laid his arm respectfully but invitingly along the top of the sofa, his hand resting behind her head, she nestled in.

He stiffened for a moment, then relaxed his hand on her shoulder drawing her closer.

"Tell me about your family," she said.

"I have a big family, two sisters and two brothers."

"In?"

"Minnesota. Most of them are in the twin cities area, but one brother is in Colorado. They are all married, three have children. The one in Colorado is gay, but even he's married and has a child now."

Star sighed. "All those weddings."

Harry nodded. "Lots of weddings. And christenings. And birthdays."

"Sounds like heaven."

They sat in silence for a moment, Star aware of every point of contact where her body pressed against his. She wanted to climb up onto his lap and wrap her arms around his neck and—

"What about you," he said, breaking into her thoughts. "You said your mom passed away. What was she like?"

It had been hard to talk about her mother since her death, but tonight Star found the words. "She was great. The original hippy. Lived life on her own terms. Valued her freedom above everything else. We lived in a Volkswagen van until I was nine, travelling around."

"That sounds cool."

"Most of the time. I learned how to read a map, make tacos and chili on a camp stove, identify the constellations, knit." She grinned. "All the important life skills."

"What happened when you were nine?"

"She tried to settle down. For my sake. We got a room in Tucson, she put me in school and got a job in a bar. We stayed there for the winter, then, in the early spring, she took me out of school and we hit the road again. I was happy to go. I hadn't really made any close friends at school." She remembered the chanting and pushing but refused to get bummed. "I was small for my age, but I was tough. I could stick up for myself.

"Anyway, that was our pattern. She'd get a job, meet a guy and things would be great for a while. I'd keep the place together, do the shopping, make my meals while she worked."

Harry's arm tightened around her shoulders. "Sounds lonely."

"Not always," she said, trying to lighten the mood. "Sometimes she could bring me to work, so there'd be music and I'd do my homework at a booth near the bar where she could keep an eye on me. It was hard to keep up with my schoolwork though, going to so many schools.

"But enough about me. Tell me about your work. It sounds exciting."

Harry shifted, not away—*don't move away*—but like he was mentally shifting gears. "It was exciting, at first, moving to Nashville at eighteen. Then we started getting gigs and that was really exciting. That was always my job, getting the gigs, making sure the guys got to the gigs, driving the van. There's a lot involved with being a travelling band besides just the music. Of course, the music is the most important thing, but I had a better head for business than Marsh and the other guys, so I handled the contracts and the money."

He stopped and stared at the flames.

"What are you going to do now?"

"Well, I'm pumped about the studio." He turned toward her, his eyes shining. "Being on the road had gotten old years ago. I'm ready to settle down, find new artists and produce their tracks. I've already found one. I'd like to do some of the mixing. I did some in the early days and loved it."

"Sounds like it could be an exciting new start."

He stared deeply into her eyes. "I'm hoping it will be."

Sensation fluttered like a moth from her throat to her chest as her heartbeat quickened. Gently, he drew her closer, and she put her hand on his broad chest, his heat surrounding her. His eyes asked the question and she smiled, let her eyelids flutter shut in surrender, and moved toward him. *Yes.*

When she touched her lips to his, a shudder went through him and she thrilled at the power she had over this sexy, fascinating man. He held back for a moment longer while she explored his lips with the tip of her tongue, then he surged into action, strong arms pulling her tight against his chest, his hand at the back of her head taking control of the angle and intensity of the kiss, and her brain ceased to function as her heart exploded.

When finally, they pulled apart, she put her fingertips to her lips, rattled to her depths, aware for the first time exactly how much damage this man could do to her heart.

Harry seemed equally shaken by the kiss and for a moment they stared into each other's eyes.

"I have to work the early shift," she said, and, always the gentleman, Harry took his cue and got her coat.

They didn't talk much on the short drive from the cottage to the cabin. Star didn't remember leaving the porch lights on that morning but was glad to see a welcoming glow over the front door.

Mostly, though, she was wondering what would happen next. Had she made an implicit promise by kissing him like that on the couch in front of the fire? The vibrations were still rolling through her body. She didn't remember *ever* having been kissed like that.

She hadn't meant to get this involved, but she wasn't thinking clearly. Didn't know the rules of his world, a world of groupies and one-night-stands.

Did he expect her to invite him in? She wasn't ready for that. Yes, she'd had boyfriends before, but they'd always been of the casual variety, the relationships only lasting a few weeks, or at most months, before they drifted apart. Casual guys with casual rules. Rules she could understand. Not intense, serious guys like Harry who'd spent the last twenty years in a world she couldn't fathom.

He took her hand and helped her down out of the SUV, then didn't let go, holding it as they walked up onto the porch, not tightly or possessively but still, she was aware in every fiber of her body of how big his hand was. How warm and steady.

By the time she got to the door, she'd changed her mind, didn't want him to let go, to set her adrift in her lonely world.

But even as she thought it, she knew that kind of thinking was dangerous. She couldn't be sucked into his magnetic field, easy as that would be. Now was the time to set up some ground rules.

She slipped her hand out of his. "Thanks for dinner, and for the ride home. I had a lovely time."

He hitched his head toward Eden, parked in the shadows behind the cabin. "Was that the same van you lived in as a child?"

She smiled. "The sum total of my inheritance."

"Didn't it used to be parked at the workshop on the other side of town?"

"You noticed?"

Harry grinned. "Hard to miss."

"I used to live over there. It isn't running right now, but I'm thinking of getting it fixed."

"How do you get to work?"

"However I can. Walk or hitch a ride."

"I'd think it would be handy to have it running."

She chewed on her bottom lip for a moment, then blurted out the truth. "It would. It's just, it's always been our get-out-of-town card, and I'm not so sure anymore that I want to go."

"Just because you get it running doesn't mean you have to leave. I'm hoping you'll stay, at least for a while."

She smiled. "I think I'll be here—for a while."

"Good." He drew her to him and she sank into the warmth of his embrace and a simple, goodnight, had-a-great-time kiss. Nothing weird or rockstar about it.

Finally he backed away, and said, "See you soon." Part statement, part question.

She nodded. *Darn right.*

Chapter 8

❄ ❄ ❄ ❄ ❄ ❄

The next day was payday, and Fiona counted the bills into Star's hand, saying, as always, "You put that in the bank. I would feel better if you would just accept a check."

And, as always, Star replied, "I will. But thank you, I prefer cash."

Then she went home and pulled a plastic bag out of the freezer. She counted out the crispy frozen bills, adding in the extra bills from this week's pay. She counted it every week, just to be sure. It was her own form of bookkeeping—minus the books. She had more than enough to fix the van and was enjoying the novelty of having a nest egg. Stability, she thought. Security. The perks of having a regular job that she had never enjoyed before. Maybe it was time to get Lorne to fix Eden, so she wouldn't have to hitch rides to work every day. Harry was right, it wouldn't mean she *had* to leave Fortune Bay right away. It just meant she *could*, when the time came, and could use it in the meantime.

Yes, that was the sensible plan. She'd call Lorne today.

She set some sandalwood incense to burn, then sank onto the floor to meditate, clearing her mind of the clutter of a day spent waiting on customers. Half an hour later, much more at peace, she began the long slow stretches of her yoga routine.

But today her concentration was jeopardized by the questions that had swirled through her head since she'd moved into the cabin. Questions about what she wanted in life. Questions she didn't know how to answer.

Finally, she shook out her limbs and settled on the couch with her knitting bag. The Christmas show was two weeks away and she wanted to finish a few more pieces to sell. She pulled out the bulky-knit red scarf she was knitting on extra-large needles, winding pieces of tinsel around the yarn every so often, pleased with the Christmas sparkle it brought to the piece. Soon she fell into the clackity-clack rhythm that always helped her think.

The small concerns of the day drifted away and left her confronted with the big question that had been on her mind since she'd been house hunting with Harry. Was this the life she wanted? Always renting, always on the move. Did she have any choice? Her eyes flicked up to where her stash lay hidden in the freezer. For the first time, she thought maybe she did have a choice. She usually gave lip service to the fact that she chose when to leave a place. But as Harry had so irritatingly pointed out, she always did leave. Why?

Because she heard her mother's voice in her head saying, *greener fields are waiting just around the corner. Let's go get 'em, Baby Girl.*

The clacking of her needles seemed to echo in the room, like another set of needles was working alongside her own.

Or maybe this is the life you want.

What? That wasn't Poppy's voice. How many people were inside her head?

She stopped knitting and sat very still, but the clickety-clack continued.

I think you heard me. Is this what you want out of life? Always on the move, never settling down?

The sound was coming from the kitchen, possibly from the vicinity of the yellow Arborite table beneath the front window. A faint glow emanated from one of the chairs, but even squinting didn't make it any clearer. She definitely heard the clacking of knitting needles though, but weirdly, the words seemed to be inside her head.

Suddenly she realized it was her turn to speak. "Uh, hi. Yes, well, I guess my life has been fine so far. Exciting, always changing. And I do have my freedom."

What freedom? Freedom's just another word...

That pushed her back a step. "You know, freedom, to pack up and leave whenever I want."

So why are you still here?

Why indeed? "I don't think I've found what I was brought here to find. I mean, there's my job, but I could walk away from it tomorrow if I found something better. But this is the nicest place I've lived in in years." Maybe ever, she thought.

The nicest place ever? Why thank you, dear, but I know it's damn cold here in the cabin in the winter.

Apparently, it didn't matter if she spoke out loud, her thoughts were heard too. But of course, if the words were inside her head... "I can handle the cold."

But a warm body beside you between the sheets wouldn't hurt.

Had she—Augusta—been listening to her thoughts all along? Ever since she'd moved in?

Don't be so shocked. I had a warm body myself once you know, and a warmer one beside me. What's holding you back?

"I saw what happened to my mother. Whenever a man came into her life, she lost her freedom. Her direction. When they'd leave, we'd hit the road again. But I always knew she was hurting."

Don't let that stop you. Hurting is part of being alive.

"Yes, but..."

Then she realized the clatter of needles had faded away, leaving Star with a panicky pressure in her chest, and more questions than answers.

She began knitting again, with a vengeance. She'd inherited this lifestyle from her mother, and a craving for freedom and the open road. Or so she thought. But maybe always being on the move was just habit, the only life she knew. She thought of herself as a master of change, but maybe what she had taken for change was just an old routine she clung to. Live for the moment, don't get too close to anyone, and when things get rough or start to press in...

Cut your losses and run.

Engrossed in her thoughts, she nodded her head. But if that was so, why wasn't she running now? Why hadn't she gotten Eden fixed and headed somewhere warmer for the winter like any sane person would do?

She had never felt in control of her life before but decided, right now, that was going to change.

Chapter 9

✻ ✻ ✻ ✻ ✻ ✻

Star hitched a ride home after work with Lily the next day, casting a wry glance at the van as she trudged down the snowy driveway. A fine powder had been falling all day. Afraid the fire in the stove had gone out, she grabbed a couple of logs off the pile as she passed. Probably less than a week's worth of wood was left at the side of the cabin. Not even a pile anymore; she was down to the last course. She'd pulled a phone number off an advertisement for firewood tacked to the community cork board in the store and would have to dip into her savings to pay for a load. Or maybe she could get away with half a load because, yes, she probably would stay for the winter in Fortune Bay.

She knelt before the open wood stove, but instead of tending the dwindling flames, she stared into the red-hot coals. Coals as hot as his kiss. A smile curled her lips as she piled kindling and one small split piece of wood on top of the glowing embers.

They had a connection, no doubt about that. She'd discovered a kind, caring guy with heat in his veins behind that polite, reserved exterior. Both their futures were up in the air right now, but she'd stay put and ride this thing with Harry out to its end, give it the winter and see where it led.

The low thrum of a motor outside the window had her closing the stove's iron door with a clang and jumping to her feet. A car door slammed in the driveway and before she could make it onto the porch, she heard voices and a thump against the outside wall. As she stepped outside, another thump. She peered over the railing and down the drive. Harry and Boz were stacking firewood on top of the dwindled pile at the side of the house.

"What are you doing? I didn't even order that yet."

Harry dropped two more logs onto the growing stack. "Last night I noticed you were low."

"I was. I am. Thank you!"

She didn't know what to say but couldn't dial down the grin as she raced inside, pulled on her jacket and boots, then ran back outside to help.

The snow was slick on the ground, covering the railing and clinging to the woodpile. She carried a couple of logs from the truck to the pile, but soon felt she was just in the way and retired to watch from the sidelines. The guys worked like a well-oiled machine and, ten minutes later, the job was done.

Harry clanged shut the tailgate and, brushing the sawdust off his gloves, came over to where she stood. She smiled to see a bright red checked shirt under his thermal vest. His cheeks were flushed from the cold and, without even thinking, she reached up and ruffled the snow off his hair. The gesture took them both by surprise and his eyes widened for a second, but then he grinned.

"Come for dinner," she said. "I owe you."

His warm brown eyes crinkled over wind-reddened cheeks. "You don't owe me, but yes, I'll come."

"It won't be Beef Bourguignon."

"French fries and a burger would be just fine. I'll take Boz home and be back in an hour?"

"Perfect."

What was she thinking! What would she serve? She mostly lived on salads and toast. Cinnamon toast, peanut butter toast, the variations were endless, but you couldn't serve capers on toast to a man like Harry.

She knew what she was thinking. She was thinking how great last night had been and how she wanted to go for round two. Her turf, her rules, and those rules might just include a tussle in her bed.

She pulled some smoked salmon out of the refrigerator and checked—*yes!*—there was spaghetti. She slipped two beers into the fridge along with a bottle of red wine, and they were in business.

She was still wearing her grease-spattered café clothes, so she raced into the bedroom and threw them off in a frenzy. What to wear? She rarely tried to look alluring, but tonight, she wanted to send a message.

There on her bed lay a form-fitting knit maxi-dress that had been her mother's. She grinned. "Good choice, Augusta." Lily was right about the matchmaking thing.

She'd never worn the dress other than to try it on when she'd gone through her mother's clothes after her death, and while the swirly red and gold design and clingy fit weren't her normal style, she'd kept it for a special occasion. Well, she thought as she slipped the soft fabric over her head, she hoped this would be a special night. And maybe, in this dress, she could channel some of her mother's sex-appeal, because her mom had beamed a sensual force out to the world that Star had never been able to imitate. In fact, she'd sometimes wondered if, as a response to Poppy's overt lustiness, she'd clamped down on her own sexuality. Well, the kiss last night had opened a new world of passion that had been swirling through her body ever since, and she planned to unleash it tonight.

When she heard the knock on the door, she froze. Then, bending at the waist, she let her unruly red mane hang loose to the floor, ruffled it with her fingers and with a motion she'd seen her mother do a hundred times, quickly straightened up, flicking her hair back into place. As she reached out to open the door, she glanced in the mirror and was pleased at the siren she saw smiling back. Then she threw open the door.

Harry stood on the porch looking much the same as he had outside a few minutes before. He'd obviously dropped Boz off and hurried right back. His eyes widened when he saw her, and she thrilled at the effect she had on him, hoping—no, sure now—she could carry it through.

He stepped inside and shrugged out of his down vest, cradling a bottle of wine. His physical presence charged the tiny room. Amazing what a checked flannel shirt could do for a city guy, instantly turning him into a man who could probably split a cord of wood and still be up for more. Not that Harry hadn't been masculine before, just very urban. She couldn't wait to run her hands down those soft flannel sleeves and up under his shirt where she knew it would be cozy and warm.

"Can I pour you a glass?" He was looking at her the same way she was sure she was looking at him, the heat blasting from his eyes threatening to burn the dress right off her body. They weren't the same safe, warm brown eyes anymore. Now they were molten chocolate, molten lava, leaving a burning trail across her chest, her cleavage, everywhere they roamed.

She gave herself a shake. "Sure. I don't have any wineglasses though. I'm just using the things that came with the cabin." She took two juice glasses out of the cupboard. "I guess Augusta wasn't much of a wine drinker."

Harry opened the wine and her eyes widened as he filled both glasses to the rim. "That's okay. I'm used to it. We rarely had the proper accoutrements on the road." He handed her a glass and took a deep swallow from his own. "We got by."

"Shall we sit? Or are you hungry?" She glanced at the window where dusk encroached as a grey fog pushed in from the water. At this time of year, it was dark by five o'clock.

"Let's sit."

He took her hand and led her to the couch. It was old velvet, soft where the springs weren't poking through. When they sat down, she fell against him, into the depression of his weight. Fine with her.

She put her wine glass on the end table, pulled her feet up under her and snuggled in closer. "I forgot to ask. Where did you get the wood?"

"Marshall got in two cords last week. All nice and dry." He grinned. "He'll never miss it."

"I should pay him back."

"My gift to you. I'd hate to think of you being cold in here, but you must be." He glanced around. "Who put up this window insulation?"

"I did." She smiled self-consciously. "The renter's best friend."

"You're okay with the woodstove?"

"I've used one many times. All last year, for starters. Another thing my mother taught me."

"She sounds like quite a lady."

"She was," Star said softly. "I feel she kind of left me a legacy to carry on our wild and free life. That's what she used to say, 'Just you and me, wild and free.'"

"And?"

"I tried, I've been wild and free—well, maybe not wild, but free—on my own for the past three years and to tell the truth, it's getting kind of lonely. Maybe I should get a dog or something.

"But I like it here. I've made some friends and Fortune Bay is starting to feel like home. I don't really want to go back on the road."

"You like living in the bush."

She smiled and nodded. "I like living in the bush. You should try it."

"I do like it. Sometimes. We had a cottage when I was a kid. I can split wood and build a fire with the best of them.

I'm just not sure it would be satisfying enough in the long run."

"You like the city." Star waited and when Harry didn't reply, she turned and looked into his face. "Don't you?"

"I'm not sure anymore. I'm not sure I know what I'm looking for. This big change-up with Marshall, and, by association my career, came out of left field. We might have gotten out of touring soon anyway, but you know, I'd have liked to have the chance to *decide* to change."

"I totally get it." She sat back in the shelter of his arm. "I think I want to change. I think I want to stay."

Her mind went back, reviewing her questions and answers and choices, until she realized his hand was caressing her neck. Then the feeling changed as his lips started moving over the sensitive spot, *right there,* just below her ear, and her body started to vibrate like a plucked string. Her hand found the soft fabric of his shirt and rubbed up and down his strong arm, the arm that was now pulling her around to face him as his lips sought hers.

Then magically, her fingers found their way under his shirt to the warmth of his firm chest, and she traced the contours, the firm abdominal muscles, the pecs, stumbling over his erect nipples and making him groan into the kiss.

His mouth dropped to her throat and he bit the skin gently making her arch her back. He pulled away and looked into her eyes. "There are no buttons on this dress."

She smiled and shook her head. *What was Poppy thinking?* "I can take care of that."

It was almost dawn before he gently kissed her goodbye at the door. In her fuzzy robe, Star sagged against the door jam, hardly able to stand, and watched him go. Then she crawled   back   into   bed.

Chapter 10
❄ ❄ ❄ ❄ ❄ ❄

Two weeks went by and Star managed to see Harry every day. And every night. They had fun times and good food by day, followed by passionate nights. Or dusky winter afternoons. The thought of that one made her blush. The phrase *hot and heavy* came to mind, and if she really thought about what it all meant, where they might be going, she would be scared. So she tried not to think, to live in the moment and enjoy the rush of emotion and heat through her body, and the blissful brain fog and heavy limbs that followed their intense bouts of love-making.

Then one afternoon, when the café rush had dwindled to the odd order of a coffee and cinnamon bun, Lily dropped by to give Star a ride home after her shift. And she had news. There was a Solstice gathering that night at Louise's and they were invited.

Star didn't want to go empty handed, so she packed up half a dozen of the muffins she'd made that day from the glass-topped case on the counter.

Louise lived half a mile past the cabin, but the night was cold and dark so Lily offered to drive.

An hour after dropping Star off at home, Lily's horn tooted in the driveway and Star rushed out between the raindrops and climbed into the car.

"What did you bring?" Lily asked.

"Fireball and muffins." Lily's laughter made Star smile and say, in her own defense, "That was all I had."

"Don't worry," Lily said. "Today was Louise's day off. I have a feeling she's been baking all day."

Lily's prophecy turned out to be true. Louise's cozy log house was warm and steamy, redolent with aromas both savory and sweet and filled with the engaging chatter of women. The kitchen and living room were lit by a multitude of candles and, remembering it was a Solstice celebration, Star felt right at home.

The winter Solstice wasn't for a few days yet, but Star's mother had taken the Solstice seriously. They didn't do Christmas, but every year, wherever they were, they attended the candlelight Solstice celebration with her mother's pagan friends. Other than the candles, there didn't seem to be any ritual about the evening tonight, which made Star relax even more. She had never been comfortable with the chanting and robes.

There would only be six of them tonight, and Star and Lily were the last to arrive. The other four were old friends but welcomed the newbies to the group. Louise was tall and model thin, her white blond hair cropped short. She had grown up in Fortune Bay and had been the cook at the café before Star. Hers had been tough shoes to fill. Louise had married Blue and had twins pretty well simultaneously the previous winter.

Frankie was Star's next-door neighbor, and had just married Sean, one of Stephanie Murphy's sons, as had Maddie, who was sitting on the rocking chair nursing a newborn.

The last guest was Stephanie herself, Star's landlady. Thirty years older than the others, she was the matriarch of the Murphy clan and seemed generally beloved by all the women. She apparently acted as a mother figure to them all, including Lily, whose father, Max, had moved in with Stephanie last week, freeing up the farmhouse. Sometimes the cross pollination of this little group made Star's head spin.

The important thing was, over the past year, they'd made

her feel at home. This was one of the things she liked most about living in Fortune Bay—the sense of community. These women were a lot of fun and seemed to embrace her, no questions asked. She felt like she could belong—and was almost ready to give it a try.

Star's stint as a bartender in Colorado Springs made her the unofficial bartender tonight. "Okay, Ladies. Tonight, I'm making a spicy Solstice drink. First ice." Three ice cubes clinked into the glass. "Then Fireball." She poured. "Just enough to float the ice cubes." A laugh went around the room. "And a squirt of lime to cut the sweetness." She held up the glass of amber liquid to the fire's light and admired the rosy glow. "Who's brave enough to try one? Or, I could add water..."

Louise took the glass out of her hand. "I need one of these after dealing with the twins all day. Thank God they're asleep." She took a long sip.

"But they're so cute," Frankie said. "When you prop them up and they bat their hands at each other."

Louise tipped her head and looked at her friend. "You sound like you're coming around on the idea of babies."

Frankie held up a hand in protest. "Give me a chance. Sean and I have only been married for a month."

"Just saying." Louise lounged back on the sofa. "The window is closing."

"Hey, I'm not as old as you guys," Frankie protested, waving vaguely across the room to where Maddie was nursing her newborn.

Star was happy to have the counter between her and this discussion of motherhood and babies and busied herself with making the drinks. It was the first time she'd been included in a group of newly married women who were also new moms, and was curious about what it was like, how these women with goals and plans and professions were handling the changes. But she didn't feel she had anything to contribute to the conversation.

When everyone had their drinks, they settled around the living room and Louise brought out platters of antipasto and—amid happy groans—chocolate brownies.

"Oh, thanks," Maddie said. "As if I'm not having enough trouble losing this baby weight."

Stephanie smiled. "It will go. Just give it a bit of time." Then she turned to Star. "How are you doing at the cabin?"

"Fine. I love it. There's so much more room to do my yoga than at Blue's shop."

"You do yoga?" Louise asked. "I need to start doing something. Carrying those fat babies around all the time has done horrible things to my back."

Maddie, who was patting the baby on her shoulder, arched her back. "I know. This little one isn't as big as the twins, but I'm feeling it anyway."

"When you're pregnant your ligaments loosen and stretch, so you can give birth. But they don't just snap back after," Star said.

Maddie nodded. "Especially not at my age. I have a daughter in college too, you know." She cradled the baby in her arms. "But Jake and I wanted to have one together."

"Last summer I worked at a spa in California and took a pre-and-post natal yoga course," Star said. "I was taking classes to get my teaching certificate. I'm not certified yet, but I could show you a few things."

"I would love that," Louise said. "But between the babies and baking for the resort—also hard on the back I might add—I don't know when I can get away."

"I can show you a few things right now that you can do *with* the babies."

"Me too?" Maddie asked. Stephanie and Louise moved the coffee table out of the way, then Star indicated that Louise and Maddie should lie down on the floor. Frankie held out her arms and took the sleeping infant.

Louise groaned as she stretched out on the carpet. "This feels great already."

Star smiled. "This is yoga too. Everything is yoga. Yoga is a state of mind. Lying here like this lets gravity realign your body, naturally. You could just lie here and let the twins crawl all over you. Or, try bringing your right knee over your left leg, letting your hips move but your shoulders stay flat on the floor. A supine twist. You can hold the knee with your left hand, if you wish, and turn you head to the left, if it feels good."

"I think that might help my lower back too," Stephanie said from where she nursed her drink on the couch. "Even if you taught a mother and baby course, I might join in."

"I can't teach," Star said hastily. "I'm not certified yet."

"We don't really care if you're certified," Stephanie said. "Not to teach at the Hall."

"I'd really need to be certified," Star protested.

"What more do you need?"

"Twenty more hours of classes."

"Twenty hours isn't much," Frankie said. "Why didn't you finish?"

The question stopped Star in her tracks. "I don't really know."

Why hadn't she finished? Probably the old getting-in-too-deep-better-cut-and-run syndrome that she was beginning to recognize as her pattern. But she was also beginning to see how cutting and running led to dead end jobs that weren't right for her, like working at the café.

Stephanie reached for a muffin and took a bite. Her eyes locked with Star's. "Baking really isn't your thing, is it dear? We'll have to try to find something that is."

"Think about running some classes," Maddie said as she got up off the floor and took back her baby from Frankie.

Star felt a flutter of excitement in her chest. "I will."

She turned to Stephanie. "I guess I should have asked,

but I put some shrink wrap over the windows at the cabin, to stop the draft."

"That's fine, dear. I know it's a hard place to heat, and it looks like we're in for a cold winter."

"I was wondering about throwing some insulation down in the attic."

The room went suddenly silent, and Star sensed she'd stepped onto dangerous ground.

"Have you taken a look up there?" Stephanie asked.

"No, but with the stairs it would be an easy job. I could just lay bats of fiberglass on the floor, maybe pour a few bags of loose insulation down into the walls from above."

Stephanie was silent for a moment, then said, "We don't like to change the attic much."

"O-kay." Star was stymied but hesitated to ask why.

Louise said. "It's kind of Augusta's domain."

Star's eyes widened. "Okay," she said with more conviction.

Louise grinned. "So, you've met Augusta."

Star shot a glance around the room.

"It's all right," Maddie said. "We all know. We've all lived there."

"I haven't," Frankie said, reaching for a brownie. "But Sean said she was responsible for the trouble he got into with my dad." She laughed. "I don't know if I believe him. I think he was quite capable of creating that mess all by himself."

"I heard her knitting," Lily said.

"Me too," Star exclaimed, glad to have her experience validated.

Stephanie nodded. "Augusta was a big knitter. She taught me."

"Well, I *saw* her." Louise said proudly.

Star felt her eyes widen again. "I saw a light, on a kitchen chair."

Stephanie looked thoughtful. "I wonder why she's still

here?"

Maddie laughed. "She must think we all need help."

Stephanie chuckled. "She always did like to—help. Some might even say, 'interfere'."

Louise sat back with a smile on her face and looked at Star. "What do you need help with?"

Nothing she wanted to talk about here. "I am looking for a new job. A new career."

Frankie reached into her handbag and pulled out an embroidered velvet bag. She undid the drawstring and pulled out an oversized deck of brightly decorated cards.

A prickle went down Star's back. She recognized those cards. Her mom was a great believer in Tarot card readings, but it seemed every time Poppy went for a reading, they moved shortly thereafter. And Star wasn't sure she wanted to move. Harry's face filled her mind, and warmth spread through her body. Not only didn't she want to move, but at this point she wanted to stay in Fortune Bay forever.

"I don't know if I should have a reading," she stammered.

"It's just for fun," Louise said.

Not always.

"We do it every Solstice," Maddie added.

Looking around the room at the encouraging faces of the group of women she longed to be part of, Star wet her lips. "I guess it couldn't hurt."

Chapter 11
❄ ❄ ❄ ❄ ❄ ❄

Star focused on the rhythmic movement of the cards as Frankie shuffled the deck and her anxiety slowly faded.

"Winter Solstice is traditionally a time of new beginnings," Frankie said. "The end of the darkness and the return of the light."

She put the deck face down on the table. "Fix a question clearly in your mind, then cut the cards."

Energy thrummed through Star's body. Excitement? Anxiety? She wasn't sure which. The burning question was, *Should I stay, or should I go?* Reminding herself that since she didn't believe in tarot readings, she had no reason to be nervous, she cut the cards.

"The cards are just an observation," Frankie said. "How you use the energy they reflect is up to you."

That alone would be a challenge since Star had rarely felt in control of her life, but now was the time. She had already decided that her new year's resolution, starting now on the Solstice, would be to take charge of her life rather than be a pawn of the universe.

Frankie reassembled the deck and tapped it twice to straighten the cards, then turned over the top three, laying them face down in a row in front of Star. "I sense you have reservations, so let's keep this simple. A three-card spread." Frankie tapped each card, beginning with the one on Star's left. "Past, present and future. We'll begin with the past."

Star turned over the left-hand card.

"Hmmm," Frankie said. "Queen of Cups. Reversed." She studied the card then looked thoughtfully at Star. "Cups rule the emotions, and love. The queen can be a woman of dreams, a nurturer and a romantic. But reversed, she can take it too far. Maybe letting emotions rule her life or nurturing to the point of not letting go." She tilted her head to one side. "I don't really think it refers to you. The past card usually refers to someone who had a profound effect on you."

Poppy. Even from the grave, Star still felt her mother's influence. The room was quiet. Everyone was watching. She nodded, mutely.

Frankie smiled. "Okay, let's move on."

Slowly and with a sense of foreboding, Star turned over the center card. It depicted a young man sitting under a tree with three cups before him. A small cloud drifted toward him. An arm stuck out of the cloud, holding another cup. This card was also upside down.

"The present," Frankie said. "The Four of Cups. Interesting. More cups. And this one is also reversed."

She smiled reassuringly at Star. "This card is about taking the time to nourish yourself, to understand what *you* need. It's about accepting love, but reversed it has the added suggestion that a new direction is open to you. And, being cups, that could be new love."

"Finally," Louise said with satisfaction. "Here we go. Anyone we know?"

Star felt herself blush and was glad for the dim, candle-lit room. She glanced at Lily, who had mentioned the day before that Harry hadn't been at the farm much and had wondered pointedly if Star knew where he'd been, even though she must have known they were spending time together. Star had dodged the question, but now could see Lily holding back a smile and hoped she wouldn't spill the beans. Thankfully, Lily could keep a secret. The previous year, during Marshall's convalescence, she'd kept his presence in Fortune Bay a secret for months.

"The future," Frankie intoned, bringing everyone's

attention back to the cards. "The Ten of Cups. More cups. More joy, fulfillment and family." She shook her head and smiled. "I love readings with happy endings. I'd say it all means, your cup is going to runneth over."

It was just a tarot reading, but it was crazy how closely it reiterated the things Star had been thinking herself lately. She shivered and looked around the candle-lit room at the faces of the women who were becoming friends, hoping there was something to these readings after all.

y z T

That night, Star couldn't sleep. She tossed and turned, plumped the pillow and flopped back down on the bed. The Solstice gathering had raised more questions than it had answered. Would it be 'settling' to settle down? Was her dream of home and family about to come true? And, most important, could she be the architect of her dreams?

Why did she feel she had to keep moving? Was it her fate or just a habit?

Or fear?

Fear? She rolled over and stared at the dark ceiling. Where had that thought come from? Her mother always told her that *they* were the brave ones, always moving on to the next adventure. The 'fraidy cats were the ones who stayed chained in one place. What could *she* be afraid of?

Love? Commitment?

She squinted in the dark at the voice in her head. "Okay, Augusta, so I do long for love, but commitment? That would be a harder step to take."

What kind of man would it take for her to drop her defenses and commit? To say the words right out loud? Not the drifters and fringe-riders she'd been thrown in with before. The other newbies in whatever-town who were only staying long enough to make some money before moving on.

It was her thing, her M.O., to leave when things became too familiar. She'd wanted that security too much as a child and had learned that whenever she let down her guard and became too invested, when she really wanted to stay, it hurt worse than ever when her mother pulled out the rug and decided it was time to pack up the van and go. Which they inevitably did. She'd learned to protect herself, to get out before she got in deep enough to care. She'd set up a repeating pattern to protect her heart, but was that how she wanted to live?

Regardless of whether it was fear or habit holding her back, it was time to take control of her destiny.

This time she wanted stability, someone responsible to share her bed and her life, who would look after her just as she would look after him. Someone with plans and dreams of his own. Someone in it for the long haul.

Was that someone Harry? She wasn't sure, wasn't sure what his plans were. Would she stay in Fortune Bay if Harry wasn't here? Thinking about all the friends she was making, she thought she might.

In the morning she woke with a burning desire to put her plans in motion. Why had she left Rocky Resort, the yoga spa she'd worked at last summer, mere hours before receiving her teaching certification? Another example of her ingrained avoidance tactics. How she avoided committing to a job, a career, when she was *this close* to achieving her goal.

She wanted to finish her yoga training and start working as an instructor. Whether here or somewhere else, it was something she could do, just for herself. She would figure out the rest of her life later.

Making a decision and following through—that was the real freedom. She'd take it one step at a time.

A running vehicle spelt freedom. Freedom to come or to go. Freedom to put her plans in motion.

She picked up her phone, called Lorne's number and

heard his message, "You know what to do."

In a firm voice, she answered. "Hi Lorne. It's time to fix the van."

Chapter 12

❄ ❄ ❄ ❄ ❄ ❄

Two days later, just before the end of Star's shift, as an early winter dusk darkened the sky, Lorne walked into the café. "Running like a top."

Getting the van back just in time to pack up her knitting for the Christmas show at the resort was a good omen. Her first decision working for her.

The next day was the day before the show, and as she worked her shift at the café she watched the trucks and vans pull into the resort driveway across the road as the larger vendors arrived to set up their elaborate booths. It was only the second year of the event, but it had been a big success the previous year and the buzz at the café counter this week promised an even greater turnout than before.

The morning of the show, Star awoke early and drove to the resort just as the watery winter dawn broke. These days the temperature was below freezing every night, but her colorful knit shawl and leg warmers made up for the lack of effective heat in the van. She pulled up with the other vendors in the line of vehicles in front of the resort entrance and began to unload amidst the cheery buzz of friendly greetings.

Max, Lily's dad, the owner and manager of the resort, held the big glass door open himself to welcome the vendors. Inside the cedar-lined, hexagonal lobby, a twenty-foot Christmas tree sparkled with colored lights and tinsel next to the stone fireplace. The delicious aromas of Louise's mince pies and Christmas cookies filled the air. Two teenage girls, Amber and Brandy, dressed as elves, were already circulating with trays of goodies for the vendors. Star grabbed her favorite, a reindeer cookie, before they all disappeared.

Noise echoed in the high-ceilinged dining hall where the sale was setting up. Just inside the door, Blue was putting the finishing touches on his display of life-sized wooden carvings of eagles and bears.

Star headed across the room, threading past the rows of tables to her booth on the side wall by the glass doors that led out to the covered patio, greeting acquaintances along the way.

She'd had good times in this room, and as she unpacked, she relived memories of last year's show and the unexpected Christmas morning invitation to the Santa brunch that followed. Also flooding back were memories of the weddings held in this space; Louise and Blue's last summer and, just a month ago, Frankie and Sean's. She felt suddenly teary. She'd been building a history here with these people and hadn't even realized it. She'd hate to leave. There were no guarantees how her life would go if she stayed, but she was going to give it her best shot.

The next two hours were filled with greeting old friends and organizing her display of colorful knit outerwear. She had been preparing for the show for a full year and had caps, scarves and shawls, one poncho and the convertible fingers-off-fingers-on mittens that she hoped would be a big seller. Two of the vendors, a jeweler and an artist in metal, came by and arranged trades for after the show, provided the items they wanted hadn't sold. At ten o'clock the doors opened, and the first buyers crowded in.

Between customers, Star used her phone to log into the resort's wifi and check out yoga retreats along the west coast where she could make up the hours she needed for her certification. An intriguing week-long session near Seattle was scheduled for the following week. Depending on her take today, she thought she might be able to afford the retreat. If need be, she could sleep in the van. It would be cold, but she'd done it before. Getting certified to teach would be a gift to herself.

Her colorful booth with its rainbow wares attracted a lot of attention, and by noon the crowd had grown to the point where she had to concentrate entirely on the shoppers. Sales were brisk.

In the middle of the afternoon, Lily, Marshall and the children arrived. Star scanned the room and her heart leapt to her throat to see Harry chatting with Blue by the door. Even in jeans and a leather jacket, Harry stood out from the crowd, in her eyes easily the most riveting man in the room.

But her heart dropped to the pit of her stomach when he put an arm around the waist of a tall woman nearby, drawing her into the conversation. She was definitely not local, in her shiny pearl pink parka with the fluffy white fur trim. It was unzipped and, even from across the room, Star could see her taut and voluptuous body outlined in a skin-tight white legging and sweater set underneath.

Harry glanced at Star and their eyes met. He didn't smile, but Star told herself that didn't mean anything, he rarely did, but still she felt like crying. He dropped his hand from the woman's waist as she picked up one of Blue's smaller carvings to study.

Star glanced away, at Lily, who had stopped by her booth. She had picked up on the scene at the door, and said, "That's Lola. An old friend." As if that explained everything.

Lola, Harry's old friend—who was, by the way, far from old—who'd come all the way to Fortune Bay to visit. And why not? Star and Harry had only been seeing each other for a few weeks and had never discussed exclusivity. Had never said their relationship was going anywhere. That was all in her mind, and she suddenly realized she'd woven, out of the spun sugar dreams are made of, a whole future with Harry here in Fortune Bay.

As he left Lola's side and made his way through the crowd toward Star's table, Lily said, "Don't worry. Lola is Marshall's friend, too. They've all known each other for years. She's married," she added as Harry arrived in front of them.

The dread trickled out of her limbs, leaving her weak and uncertain. After all, what did she know about Harry's past? Just a vague image of 'life on the road' that she'd conjured in her own imagination.

Then he came around behind the table and gave her a light brush of his lips on her cheek, and she turned into such a puddle of lust and desire that it only deepened her fear about what was to come.

He tied a rainbow-colored scarf around his neck. "You need me to model your wares?"

She grinned. This was not the scarf she was making for him for Christmas. She wasn't a total idiot. His was a subtle blend of black and brown with thin red stripes, something more suited to his circumspect personality. But she loved that he'd wear her raucous scarf here, in public, at the show. A serious, Harry-style joke.

Lily had gone to find Lola and soon brought her over to the booth. With Harry beside her behind the table, Star soon relaxed in the glow of Lola's enthusiasm over her rainbow legwarmers.

"These are so cool! Just what I've been looking for. They'd be so much fun for après ski this winter. How many do you have? A bunch of us are going to Aspen for the holiday. I'd buy half a dozen for my girlfriends for Christmas. All different, of course."

Star smiled. "They are all different."

"One of a kind," Lily added.

"Do you have a website?"

Star opened her mouth to say she didn't even have a computer, but Lily cut in. "We're working on it."

Lola held a scrunchy pair up against her white leggings. "I bet they're a big seller at this time of year."

She took six pair, and as Star swiped her credit card on the app on her phone, her dream of attending the yoga retreat became more of a reality.

"Come for dinner?" Lily asked as their party prepared to leave.

Harry put an arm around Star's waist and kissed her cheek, warming her to her core.

"Of course."

Chapter 13
❋ ❋ ❋ ❋ ❋ ❋

Dinner in the kitchen at the farm was a loud and relaxed affair. Star sat back and watched as Harry joined in the good-natured ribbing with his old friends. This was the guy she was falling in love with, but something was still strained between them, something unsettled.

After dinner, Marshall pulled Harry into the living room to hear the new chorus of the song he was working on, leaving the women sitting together over their wine at the kitchen table.

Lily told Lola about the yoga retreats she and Star were planning, and Lola told them about the yoga holidays she went on with her après ski girlfriends. "They're a big thing these days, you know," she said, extending her long legs to admire her new legwarmers.

Star smiled. "I know. I used to work at a spa in northern California. Rocky Retreat."

"I've been there," Lola exclaimed. "All the girls in L.A. go on retreats. To get away from the guys and just chill out."

Lily caught Star's eyes and asked, "What do you do at a retreat?"

"Some Yoga," Lola replied. "But that's not all. Depends where and what time of year. You need a hook, a great location or a famous chef or something. This place would be perfect."

"That's what I was thinking," Lily said. "My Dad wants to expand the resort. He's planning on building a conference center in the spring to hold retreats and weddings and public functions, like today's show. Holding them in the dining room is too disruptive."

"That would be perfect," Lola said. "I could fill up your

first one, no problem."

She stood up and stretched. "I'm just going to check in with the guys and see if Harry's ready to go back to the resort."

Lola needed a ride. With Harry. Of course. Although Star had gotten to know Lola better over dinner, it was still hard to keep that saucy green dragon on a leash.

A few minutes later, Harry strolled into the room. He leaned over Star, putting both hands on the arms of her chair, his body offering them a modicum of privacy, and said in a low voice, "I should take her, but I can come back. Or you could come with me."

Their faces were inches apart, and Star lost concentration as she stared into his warm brown eyes. She was losing her independence with this man. Losing her mind. Time to take a step, a tiny step, back. She smiled. "It's okay. It's been a long day, and I told Fiona I'd work in the morning."

His lips touched hers in a quick kiss, more of a peck really, she thought with a sting of disappointment. Then he was gone.

Shortly after they left, Star made her exit too, driving Eden down one lane and then the next to the cabin where the porch light was shining a welcome. She knew she hadn't left it on, in fact she distinctly remembered turning it off when she'd left this morning before dawn. It happened all the time, and she'd come to think of it as Augusta's way of saying, "Welcome home".

Although she was tired, she was too wound up from the busy day at the show to sleep, and her new plans swirled in her mind. She wished Harry was here to bounce ideas off, but during the past few days she had felt her independence slipping away. Now that she had her van back, she needed to regain the feeling of freedom she always felt when her escape hatch was primed and ready to go.

But this time she would use it constructively, to move her

dreams ahead. There was one space left in the five-day course being held at a mountain retreat just outside Seattle. It was billed as a way to chill out during the often crazy, pre-Christmas week, and that sounded great to her. It was always an awkward week. When her mother was alive, they hadn't celebrated Christmas, although she'd always secretly wished they could. She suspected Lily would invite her to join them for dinner, and she would, but just as a guest. It was okay, she was used to that. After all, she'd celebrated the season on the Solstice with the women the other night at Louise's, and at the Christmas Sale today, so anything else holiday-related was a bonus.

That evening after Lola and Harry had left, she and Lily had brainstormed Lily's idea for holding yoga retreats at the resort, and that discussion was circling in her head, too. She fired up the stove, made herself a cup of herbal spice tea and grabbed her knitting. Time to finish the grey and red scarf she was making for Harry that she'd set aside in the push to finish pieces for the show. She hoped he would be here for Christmas but had no assurance. They hadn't had time alone today to talk, but she hoped they would make plans for the holiday tomorrow.

Settling into the big comfy chair by the woodstove, she mulled everything over, the clack of her needles a background to her thoughts. Fortune Bay was the ideal spot to run a retreat. Besides the natural beauty, the resort offered the perfect accommodation—sophisticated amenities with a rustic ambiance—for a yoga getaway. They could offer hiking and biking on the trails and, in summer, swimming and boating. They'd design a delicious menu of healthy food for the participants, with a special 'goodbye' splurge on the last night. Lily excelled at organizing special programs and events, and Star was confident that together they could make this work.

Quit stalling.

She nodded and set her knitting aside. Her job was to get her ass certified. She checked the time. It wasn't too late. She reached for her phone.

Chapter 14
❇ ❇ ❇ ❇ ❇ ❇

The following morning, Harry took Lola to SeaTac airport, a two hour drive each way. When he returned to the resort, he couldn't settle down, so he walked a snowy path along the lake, across a creek and through the forest, pounding out his frustration with each footstep.

His thoughts were in a state of constant turmoil these days. Seeing Lola had brought the old life back in detail. Marshall may have always been the star, but Harry was used to being in charge. *He* decided when they would come and when they would go, where the next gig and the next meal would be. When they would take time off and when they would start working again.

Now Marshall was making decisions on his own, and Harry understood that Marsh had his family to look out for and that of course he should make the decisions regarding them. But the decision to open the studio was a joint business venture, yet Marshall seemed to be making all the decisions. Bad decisions in Harry's opinion. Decisions based on his heart.

Fortune Bay might be a nice place for a cottage—but it was no place to set up a studio. Marshall had bought the large house Star had found on the lake. He could easily afford it—as could Harry for that matter, if he wanted to, and, in fact, he was seriously considering buying the house next door— the smaller house he had looked at with Star—*as a cottage.* His thinking became fuzzy as he remembered the joy in her eyes as she imagined living there. Her life, so far, sounded lonely and unstable, and he thought she might seriously be considering settling down.

Considering. She hadn't said she'd decided to stay, just that she wanted to. She wasn't happy with her job, that much was clear, but in her position, you go where the jobs are, and there weren't many jobs in this little resort town.

And hadn't they both said they weren't ready to settle down yet? He frowned as he stared at the ground beneath his feet as he walked, not really seeing the fir trees and the rushing creek as he passed. His fear was that one day he'd walk down the lane to the cabin and the van would be gone. She would be gone. For good.

This past couple of weeks had awakened a place in his heart he hadn't known existed. A place of peace and the joy of just seeing her face. And the sex. Well, the sex was amazing. He hadn't known he could feel that way. Afterwards, holding her, he felt overwhelmed by a contentment he had never experienced before. He'd be crushed when it ended, and that was another reason not to let his imagination get the better of him.

Suddenly he found himself at the farm, not entirely sure how he'd gotten there. He stamped the snow off his boots at the back door and let himself in.

Marshall was at the electric keyboard in the living room, engrossed in his process. That was good to see, but they had to get this decision about the studio location hammered out now, before they got in any deeper. "Marsh, can we talk?"

Marshall looked up at Harry as if awakening from a dream and gave his head a shake as he came back to the real world. After twenty-five years of friendship and working together, Harry understood Marshall's habits and gestures, and gave him a minute to reconnect to the world.

"What's up?"

"We have to get this worked out for once and for all." At Marshall's confused look, Harry threw up his hands. "Where are we going to set up the studio, Marsh?"

"Here. I want to have it here."

"We can't have it here. There's no infrastructure."

"We don't need infrastructure to make music. Instruments, a building, recording equipment, sure. But what could be better than that building in the forest? Can't you see it? Big windows looking out into the trees? The music will have a special sound, coming from an environment like that."

"That's bullshit."

Marshall looked at the keyboard for a minute, put his hands on the keys and played a few chords. "I can't go back, Harry. I *can't* go back." He held up his hands, the left one difigured with unnaturally smooth, post-surgical skin stretched across it. "I have to start over, not be reminded of my old life at every turn. I've been blessed with a chance to begin again, and I mean to take it. Here, with my family, in Fortune Bay."

"You're thinking with your heart, not your head."

Marshall looked him in the eye, a long deep stare. "You should try it, Harry. It feels good to live by your heart."

Shaken by his words, Harry suddenly understood for the first time that Marshall was not coming back. That Harry would have to embrace this new life or go it alone in L.A.

Then Marshall continued. "I want you here with me. The studio..." He shook his head. "I can't do it without you."

Harry was silent. "Jeeze, Marsh." He turned his head and looked out the window. They'd been together since they were kids. Had they finally come to a parting of ways?

"And what about Star?" Marshall asked.

Her name was like a burning arrow shot into his heart. Leaving would mean more than leaving Marshall and their history—now it meant leaving Star, too. But he couldn't show this soft side to Marshall. Never had. "What about her?"

"I thought she might be an added incentive for you to set up here."

"She's not a permanent factor. I doubt if she'll stay for

more than a few more months, or weeks. I can't make a decision based on her."

"Have you told her how you feel?"

Harry blew out a long breath, "No, I haven't. And I'm not going to. We'll see how it goes but no, I don't see any happy endings there. We're too different."

"She could be the one."

That was the last straw. "The one? You're getting soft, Marsh. And why are you suddenly calling the shots? Telling me what to do with my life?" He spun around and headed for the door. "I have to get out of here, to think. I'm going back to L.A."

"See if you can line up the equipment we need while you're there," Marshall called to Harry's retreating back.

Chapter 15
❋ ❋ ❋ ❋ ❋ ❋

"I need some time off," Star said.

Fiona looked up from where she knelt stocking the shelves, the felt reindeer antlers on her headband bobbing. "Thanks for the heads up. When are you thinking?"

"Right away. Tomorrow. I know it's the week before Christmas and things will be busy, but there's a course I want to take in Seattle. It ends Christmas Eve. I could work all the shifts after that to make up, opening on Boxing Day. Terry could take a few days off then."

"You go, dear. We'll take care of the café."

Star went back to work with a new determination. Her life was on track, but she still wondered—she laughed, was more like was *consumed* by the question—what was Harry going to do? Would he stay, or would he go?

Their relationship wasn't on a level where she felt she could ask, but then again, if they were just friends she *would* ask. Now that they were clearly more than friends, new rules seemed to apply and that was totally confusing. She didn't want to push, pushing could backfire, but she really wanted to know.

She'd told him she planned to try to stay in Fortune Bay. Hopefully she meant enough to him that it would influence his decision. They had been spending so much time together and it had been so good. She thought—hoped—their relationship meant as much to him as it did to her.

Meant as much—why couldn't she be honest with him and just come out and say it? She was crazy about the guy. He was gorgeous and kind and thoughtful and responsible— what more could you ask? He exuded strength, and she felt safe with him. She thought they would be good together, maybe even make a life together—but she wouldn't push him into anything. His life was up in the air and he had to make the decisions that were right for him. She just hoped they included her.

All she could do was work on her own plans and let him know how she felt. But definitely, no pushing.

He walked into the café and her chest filled with so much happiness that she could scarcely breathe. But her smile dissolved when she saw the serious look on his face. Not just serious, but withdrawn. The old, distant Harry was back, and fear pierced the balloon of joy that was her heart until it deflated back to its old, hard, practical state. Just pumping the blood through her body but not feeling the love.

He sat on a stool. She poured him a coffee and tried to smile. "Hi, handsome."

When he didn't return her smile, ice crept into her blood. He stared into his coffee and spoke. "I wanted to let you know, I'm going back to L.A. For a while."

Her cheeks hurt in an effort to keep smiling. "Are you coming back?"

His deep brown eyes looked into hers, searching. "Do you want me to?"

Her face froze. Did she? Of course she did. They were almost a couple, things had been going so well, she wanted to move on into her daydreams of them in the house—yes, she had been thinking about the house—with children and dogs and—

But then she'd be stuck. If he came back for her she'd feel obligated to stay and fulfil whatever dreams *he* had, and his dreams may be nothing like what she was thinking—

"Sure."

He looked confused. "Sure?"

She upped the smile—surely the fakest smile that wouldn't fool anyone, certainly not Harry whose eyes seemed to see into her soul. "Of course I do."

His beautiful brown eyes winced, almost imperceptibly. She knew she'd hurt him, but she was panicked by the enormity of saying *yes*. Of taking the big step into a future together. And, she thought, her eyes growing wide with uncertainty, he hadn't asked her to. Had he?

"When are you coming back?" she asked again.

He held her gaze for a long moment, and with a rush of hope, she thought he would say something to let her know how he felt. Instead, he said, "I don't know."

Well, that pretty well said it all, didn't it? He was going. *It's been fun.* Just as she'd suspected at the start, she was just one of the girls he knew on the road.

Leaving his coffee untouched he stood up again and now she thought she saw a hint of vulnerability beneath his brusque demeanor. "I'll come back, but I don't know what's in the cards for me. I—" his voice broke and he gave his head a little one-two shake. "I can't promise you anything."

She pressed her lips together. *Don't go!* But he had to make up his own mind. "I'll be here."

He nodded, then leaned across the counter and gave her a quick kiss on the cheek. No hug, no soulful look, just a *see you later*, and he was out the door.

The fake smile faded, and she slumped against the counter, empty inside, as if all the life had been sucked out of her.

Then, after a moment, she pulled herself up. *I've been through this before. This is my cue to pack up and go.*

Her mom was right: they were the free ones. They could carry on.

Her van was ready, but this time she wouldn't run. This time she had a plan and, with or without him, she'd stick to it.

After her shift ended, she drove back to the cabin and threw her yoga clothes into her pack. She turned the light off on the front porch. She'd be gone for five days and planned to come back ready to start a new phase.

Her life, her plans.

Chapter 16
* * * * * *

After the painful leave-taking with Star, Harry drove two hours straight, back to the airport for the second time that day, telling himself it was better this way. Time to get his life back on track and not lose his heart to a woman who had never committed to anything in her life.

The drive gave him time to think. To think about how he was right, and Marshall was wrong. Dead wrong. He could picture it clearly, his dream studio, in the valley, high tech and tuned in, not some artsy commune in the woods that Marshall seemed to think everyone in the industry would flock to.

He *would* look at equipment, because he was doing this anyway, his way, regardless of whether Marshall was in or out.

He caught the first flight to the City of Angels and picked up his Porsche at LAX, cruising home through the light, late night traffic.

Unlocking his apartment door, he stepped into a silent shadowy world where lights of the city below reflected off the living room ceiling onto the glass and chrome furniture. He flicked on the light in the foyer, a room as big as the living room at his cottage in Fortune Bay, and hung his jacket in the closet. Running his hands over his chest, he realized he was still wearing the red flannel shirt, and his heart twisted as he remembered the last time he wore it—Star's hands pressed against his chest as they kissed.

He unbuttoned the shirt and took off the jeans and dumped them both in the hamper. He hadn't brought any luggage back from Fortune Bay. He didn't need any. He walked into his closet and flicked on the light. Rows of shirts and jackets hung on the left, pants and shoes on the right. Everything he'd need for a couple of weeks in the city. That would give Marshall time to think things over and realize that Harry was right.

He chose a soft blue button-down shirt and a casual pair of slacks, and then prowled the apartment; no food in the refrigerator, nothing to watch on TV. Soon he found himself back in the living room staring out the window on the city below.

Lola had told him when he'd driven her to the airport that she was having a Christmas party that night, before she left for Aspen tomorrow. Harry glanced at his watch—ten o'clock. Not late for a Hollywood party.

When he arrived, he handed his keys to the valet in the circular drive and walked toward the low sleek house. It wasn't a very big party, not by Lola's standards. The sixty-degree night felt positively balmy after the cold damp Pacific Northwest, and he wondered for the hundredth time why Marshall wanted to live in Fortune Bay.

The door was open, and he let himself in. The foyer was decorated in silver and blue lights with three dimensional lustrous black stars hanging from the ceiling. A giant Christmas tree in the living room echoed the color scheme, which didn't scream *Christmas* to Harry but must be this year's latest thing.

The noise level was a comfortable din. Lola had called it a gathering of her and her considerably older husband's closest friends. Harry went straight to the bar and ordered soda and lime with ice, quickly, before someone put something stronger in his hand, then looked around the room.

Lola had been with them for years on the road as a back-up singer and had appeared in a few of Marshall's videos, so Harry knew half the people in the room. He schmoozed from one group to the next, asking about up-coming projects, trying to keep his foot in the door and his name on the table in case they actually got this studio project off the ground.

Everyone asked about Marshall, as they'd been doing now for over a year, and Harry told them he was doing well, enjoying his down time with his family, and laughingly told one group he'd moved to Fortune Bay.

"Lucky guy," one burnt-out musician about his own age commented.

"I'm heading home tomorrow," his buddy, a guitar player, said. "West Virginia. Can hardly wait."

Harry couldn't help but ask, "Nice for a holiday, but full time?"

"I would if I could," the guitarist said.

It seemed everyone was going home for the holidays. Over the two days that followed, Harry tried to get down to work—people to see, places to go—but it wasn't easy to connect in that week before Christmas, even in L.A.

He did manage to meet with a small recording studio in Venice Beach that was shutting down. They were selling off all their equipment, virtually everything he and Marshall would need to get started. A windfall.

"Why are you selling?" Harry asked.

"We just can't make a go of it," the owner, a young guy with multicolored spiked hair replied. "Expenses are too high. The rent is killing us."

"Where should we ship it?" his partner asked.

Harry had shaken his head. "Don't know yet. My partner, Marshall Mason, wants to set up in a small town on a lake up north, but I don't see how that will work."

"Could be a great idea. People like to get out of the city. Get some peace and quiet, to write and record."

"But if you couldn't make a go of it here..."

"You'll have it made with your connections, man. Just let

us know where to ship it when you decide."

But Harry didn't look for a location. Somehow, in the past two days, he'd lost momentum. Last night he'd met a few old friends, performers they'd come up with, for drinks at a bar— something he usually tried to avoid, knowing it could become a dangerous habit. They sounded interested in the studio idea, and damned if they didn't all say they'd love a chance to get out of the city and record somewhere like Fortune Bay.

"Splendid isolation," Clancy James, a *Billboard* phenomenon, called it.

On the third afternoon, Harry sat on the black leather sofa in his apartment, drinking a beer and watching the city lights blink on below.

He'd hoped to firm things up with the kid they'd signed to start work on a new album in February, but he was in Louisiana with his family. Harry's own parents were in St. Kitts with his brother's family for the holiday. In October, they'd invited him to go with them, but he had declined, thinking he'd have better things to do. That was a laugh.

He could go out, of course. He knew a few places where he'd probably run into some people he knew, but that was already getting old. His apartment felt like dead space to him now. Always had, come to think of it. Just a place to store his skis and dirt bike between tours. The thought of working in the city and coming back to this cold apartment every night scared him.

That wasn't a life. Maybe Marsh was right. A life was built around the people you spent it with. It didn't matter where you worked. Since he'd been back in the city, a studio in the forest had taken on a certain weird appeal, if it meant he could be with the people he loved.

Twenty-seven stories over the city, the view was just a panorama of buildings and lights. He was up too high to make out any of the people below. In a city of four million people, he felt completely alone. They might call it The City of Angels, but his angel was back in Fortune Bay.

Everywhere he went he was faced with reminders of Christmas, and of the people he'd rather be spending it with. Marshall and the kids always welcomed him, but it was their space, not his. Now more than ever, since Marsh had found Lily. And Harry had found Star.

He shook his head. He'd turned his back on all of them. What an idiot.

Suddenly he realized why he'd never felt at home in Fortune Bay. It was because he didn't have a home. And, without Star, he didn't have a future.

They needed a home of their own.

He took off his blue pinstripe shirt and pressed pants and dug his jeans and flannel shirt out of the hamper. He hadn't been in town long enough to have them laundered, but gave them a shake and a perfunctory sniff and decided they would do. He'd go back and apologize. Tell her he was crazy about her and he wanted to give it a go.

With that thought burning in his mind, he grabbed his jacket and the keys to his SUV and was out the door.

He drove all night and at noon the next day he was back in Fortune Bay, driving past the resort and Marshall's farm, to the cabin. Icicles decorated the fir branches that hung over the snow-covered lane. His heart was raw with need by the time the ramshackle building came into sight—but then he realized there were no tracks in the snow. And the crazy hippy van wasn't in its spot behind the cabin. His worst fear had come true. Star was gone.

Not ready to believe it, he walked up onto the porch and banged on the front door, but knew in his heart it was futile. No lights shone inside; no smoke issued from the chimney.

Hurrying back to the car, he drove frantically to the farm. Marshall looked up from his keyboard in surprise and smiled when Harry barged in through the front door.

"You're back."

"I'm back. Where is she?"

"Who? Lily?'

"No. Star."

Marshall's brow contracted in a thoughtful frown. "I don't know. At work? I haven't seen her in a few days."

Of course. She'd be at work. She'd gotten the van fixed and was driving it to work. He just hadn't seen it when he passed the store, so fixed was he on getting to the cabin. *She said she'd be here.* She wouldn't have packed up and gone.

But in his panicked mind he also heard her say, *the van is my get-out-of-town card.* And it was his fault if he'd made her play it by storming around like an idiot, not able to say the words, *I love you.*

The VW wasn't at the general store either and, although he went in to check, he knew by the sinking feeling in the pit of his stomach that she wasn't there. He got back in the car and drove, unthinking, until he found himself driving down the long, snow covered driveway to the cottage on the lake that he and Star had found together.

At the end of the drive, he stopped and studied the house. Icicles hung from the gingerbread trim on the porch and eaves, enhancing its fairytale charm. He remembered Star's excitement when she saw it. Her dream house. She'd been enamored of it, right from the start, and he had to agree, it was perfect for Star. Perfect for them.

Of course, it would need a big addition on the back, opening up those ridiculously small upstairs back bedrooms. Kids needed more space than that. And a big family room behind the kitchen where they could spend evenings and Christmases to come.

He did a quick three-point turn, almost getting stuck in the snow, and booted it down the drive.

But where was she? He'd blown it by leaving like that. Now she was freaked and had probably turn tail and run.

He knew her issues with settling down. He should have been more sensitive. Moved more slowly. But he'd never been Mr. Sensitivity. He gripped the wheel. It wasn't too late to learn.

He'd find her, wherever she'd gone. Find her and bring her back. He winced. There was that famous Harry Brewster sensitivity again. He'd find her and *ask* her to come back to him.

Hell, he'd *beg*, if that's what it took.

Chapter 17
❄ ❄ ❄ ❄ ❄ ❄

On Christmas eve, Star climbed out of the van, smiling fondly as Augusta flickered the porch light in welcome. It had been a good week, but she was glad to be home. Her body ached from stretching muscles she'd forgotten she had, but she had gotten her hours, and her certificate. The hands-on training with the other participants had left her inspired to begin teaching a class. Teaching would make her keep studying and growing herself, learning new methods to pass on to her students.

Tugging Adam and Eve aside, she reached into the van for her pack, slung it over her shoulder and slowly climbed the steps to the porch.

The cabin was cold. No one had lit a fire for her this time. As she knelt before the woodstove and crumpled paper from the bin, her thoughts turned to Harry, again. She'd felt terrible about how they had left things when he came to the café to say goodbye. The first day of the retreat, it had been hard to concentrate on the practice. As the classes wore on she got into the groove but spent every night thinking about him. About them.

Her mind had been on Harry the whole way back. She was praying he'd come back for Christmas. The going was slow as she wove her way through the small towns on her route, the main streets full of people hurrying to finish their Christmas preparations. As darkness fell, the towns lit up, the stores bedecked with a rainbow of lights. She stopped for a woman crossing the road, holding tight to her daughter's hand. Behind her, a man in a bulky scarf, the bags in his arms almost obscuring his face. For one brief moment, she thought it was Harry. But no. He was in L.A.

She wanted this small-town life, but she also wanted to give her relationship with Harry a chance. And he'd made it clear Fortune Bay wasn't for him, so if that's what it took, she was willing to give L.A. a shot. The City of Angels. How bad could it be?

With the fire in the woodstove set, she struck a match and moments later the kindling was ablaze.

They were both such dummies, particularly her, skirting the issues, not trusting herself to tell him how she felt. She just hoped it wasn't too late.

It's never too late. Augusta's voice rang clear in her head. *But sometimes men need prodding. Straight talk.*

It was true, she hadn't been clear with him. She hadn't told him she wanted to stay in Fortune Bay, that she had business plans, life plans, and that she hoped he'd be there too.

She got to her feet. She'd go to Lily and Marshall's. They'd know where he was. He might even be there already, this being Christmas eve.

She pulled her new parka back on and slipped on the warm, waterproof boots she'd treated herself to in the city. She'd need them both if she was going to stay.

A snowstorm had blown through while she'd been away, and she walked in the tire tracks back out to the road, fresh snow on the low hanging branches of the trees sparkling in the beam of her flashlight. When she got to the main road, a few snowflakes began to fall. Across the snowy field, a warm light spilled from the farmhouse windows.

She wanted a home and family, too. Declaring your goals to the universe and letting the universe take it from there was something she'd learned from her mother. She'd learned a lot of good things from Poppy, but lately she'd realized how different they were, that they had different goals. Star would always love her free-spirited mom, but she had to hike her own trail. Starting now.

The time had come to say it out loud. She stopped and said, "I want to stay."

She grinned. It felt good to make a firm declaration, so she added, in an even louder voice, "I want a home and family of my own."

She inhaled a cold, invigorating breath and, in the middle of the dark road, raised her face to the falling snow and shouted, "I love you, Harry Brewster!"

She didn't know what she expected to happen, but having just shared her hopes and dreams with the universe, she would have thought there'd be a little more feedback than the silence that followed. All she heard was the sound of the wind in the trees, the faint shushing of waves on the shore. And the crunch of tires, coming toward her on the gravel road.

Headlights came around the corner and she stepped out of the middle of the road. A black SUV slowed to a halt beside her and soundlessly the window rolled down.

Harry. Hot tears squirted in her eyes. "I thought you weren't coming back," she said. "I really thought you weren't coming back." She wiped her nose with the back of her mitten.

He jumped out of the car and lifted her feet off the ground in a bear hug and bear kiss that she hoped would never end.

When they came up for breath, he put her back on solid ground and with his arm around her shoulders, led her to the passenger door. "Of course I came back. I just had to figure a few things out." His voice cracked a little when he said, "I thought *you* weren't coming back." Then he kissed her, hard, and opened the car door. "Now get in. I have something to show you."

Her head was so full of the things she wanted to tell him that she scarcely noticed the thousands of Christmas lights as they drove through the village.

To her surprise, he asked, "How was your course." Then he grinned and added, "Lily told me."

She told him about her week, the yoga course and her new teaching certificate. She wasn't sure what his reaction would be when she got to the part about the plans she'd made with Lily for retreats at the resort, but his face broke into a grin. "Sounds like you're planning to stay."

"I want to stay," she said. The honesty had to start now. "I want to settle down. But the 'where' is negotiable, as long as it's with you."

"I feel the same way. We'll work it out." He took her hand and held it on his lap, and they grinned at each other in the darkened car, their faces lit by the soft blue glow of the dashboard lights.

When he turned down the driveway to the cottage by the lake, Star's heart started beating double time. She sucked in an excited breath. "What are we doing here?"

Harry's smile broadened but he didn't reply until the car had come to a halt. He opened her door and she leapt into his arms. Then he set her gently on her feet, facing the house.

"It's for you. I bought it, for you. For us. I hope it's what you want because I want this. A home, with a fire in the fireplace, stockings hanging from the mantel, and you in the kitchen making Christmas cookies." Tears welled in his eyes. "I want it all. The whole shebang. I love you Star."

She threw herself into his arms and he lifted her effortlessly off the ground. "I love you too. This place is perfect. I could see us here together from the moment we found it."

"Wait a minute," he said.

What more could there be? But he reached into his pocket, pulled out a small device and pointed it toward the house. Suddenly, the cedar tree beside the porch sprang to life with lights of red and gold.

Star laughed. "I love it. It's the perfect yard for kids, and dogs." She covered her mouth but couldn't hide her smile. "I hope you want kids and dogs."

He nodded seriously. "At least two. Of each."

Then, she took a step away, held out her arms and fell backwards into the knee-deep snow. Careful to leave a clean impression, she swished her arms and legs in an arc. Then she held up her hands, he pulled her to her feet, and they both looked down at the imprint she'd left in the snow.

"A perfect Christmas eve angel," she said.

"You're my Christmas angel. I want to share a life with you—starting with this house."

Now *she* had tears in *her* eyes, but she smiled through them. "This is the best Christmas ever—my first Christmas ever."

He took the house keys out of his pants pocket. They were warm as he pressed them into her hand. "Starlight, honey, it's you and me."

She grinned in reply. "Wild and free."

Read on for a sneak peek at
the first book in the
Fortune Bay series,
Summer of Fortune

Summer of Fortune

Book One in the Fortune Bay series

by

Judith Hudson

MAY

Chapter 1

When life hands you lemons, you make lemonade.

My motto in life, thought Maddie Tedesco when her ex-husband's name popped up on the caller display. But really, how much lemonade did one woman have to drink?

When she answered the phone, his greeting was brief. "Maddie."

"Mark."

They didn't spend much time on pleasantries anymore. He was Jenny's father though, so when he asked to speak to their daughter, Maddie handed her the phone.

"Hi Dad...Everything's great...No, nothing planned ..." Jenny's voice rose to a shrill crescendo. "I'd love to... Sure, we'll talk." She put down the phone with a satisfied smack.

Listening from her post at the kitchen sink, Maddie's jaw clenched. How many times had Mark disappointed their daughter, making plans and then not showing up? If he did it again, she'd wring his neck.

Plastering the smile on her face that she'd perfected in the ten years she'd been divorced, she turned to her daughter.

"Mom. You'll never guess what. Dad asked me to spend the summer with him and Kate."

Maddie's cheeks stiffened as the smile melted like a chalk drawing in the rain. Jenny would graduate from high school next spring and, thorny as it may be, this could be her last summer at home. By asking Jenny first, Mark had undermined Maddie's veto again, swooped in like a fairy godfather and invited Jenny to Yuppiedom-by-the-sea.

Maddie leaned heavily on the counter. "Do you want to go?" Her voice sounded hoarse.

"Of course I do. Why would I spend the summer in this stifling attic when I can be in a mansion by the beach?"

Hardly a mansion, but Mark's beautiful Seattle Craftsman-style home *was* right across the street from the beach, and a far cry from Maddie's third floor walk-up.

"How about it, can I go?" Jenny asked.

"I don't know. I have to think…"

"Come on. This is my chance to move up in the world. I don't want to end up like you—living in an attic when I'm thirty-five. "

"Hey, it's cozy."

"And working at a job I hate."

"I don't hate my job," Maddie objected. But Jenny had pretty well nailed it. Being a receptionist at an art gallery—or an administrative assistant, as Maddie preferred to call it—wasn't her dream job, but it did pay the rent.

"You could have fooled me." Jenny put her hands on her hips in a perfect imitation of Maddie. "You always say I can achieve whatever I want if I just put my mind to it. 'Go after what you want,' you say. Well, I want this. A chance for something better."

Maddie stared at her daughter. Jenny stared boldly back, her long, straight, reddish-blonde bangs hanging in her eyes. Maddie's hand itched to reach out and brush them aside but she resisted. Instead, she turned away, picked up a scrub pad and began scouring the sink. "We'll see."

As she sensed Jenny watching her from the door, her shoulders stiffened and her hand slowed in the sink.

"It's clean enough Mom," Jenny said softly. Then, like a wraith, she vanished into her room.

Maddie put her hands on the counter, dropped her head and sunk her weight into her arms. It was unnerving when Jenny caught her cleaning. And really, was cleaning so bad? Jenny seemed to think so but Maddie could think of things that were much worse.

She had promised herself she'd be a good role model for her daughter, the best mother ever. Fun yet patient, adventurous yet wise. Her daughter's best friend. And it had worked, at first. But sometime during the last few years, their relationship had gone from BFFs to combatants. Mark could offer Jenny a life Maddie couldn't hope to achieve. What if Jenny didn't want to come back after the summer?

She glanced at the clock, six thirty, time for a family-fix.

In the living room she turned on the TV and the *Family Ties* opening scenes appeared on the screen. As always, the reassuring music was an anchor for her turbulent emotions. Turning up the volume, she went back to the kitchen to start dinner.

These were the families she'd grown up with: The Seavers, the Cosbys and her favorite, the Keatons. Elyse Keaton had been her dream mother, had taught her more about being a mother than her own mom ever had. Despite being an architect, Elyse always had time for the family.

Maddie longed to be part of a family like that and had tried to give Jenny the best home she could. But obviously her best wasn't good enough or Jenny wouldn't be so eager to go and live with her dad.

Elyse's voice echoed in her head. *"Of course Jenny wants to connect with her father. Don't you remember what that was like?"*

She remembered all right. The longing, the wondering, the ache in her chest. At least Jenny knew who her father was.

Maddie let out a sigh that left her hollow. The weight of inevitability settled on her shoulders. Of course Jenny should go to her dad's. It was the right thing to do.

Go after what you want. She *had* said that—and meant it. Maybe in this case, being a good mother meant letting her daughter go.

Wiping her hands on a dish towel, Maddie called Jenny back into the kitchen. Maddie's heart twinged when she recognized the suspicious look on her daughter's face that pretty well epitomized their past year together.

She tried to smile but her cheeks felt like hard plastic. "I've made a decision. You can go to your dad's for the summer."

Jenny let out a whoop and threw her arms around her mother. The irony wasn't lost on Maddie that this was the first spontaneous hug in so long, and all because she was letting her go.

Jenny rushed to her room to call her friends. Maddie took a deep breath and turned back to her magazine recipe. She'd splayed the chicken on a roasting pan—apparently it baked faster this way—and now crumbled the dried rosemary and thyme between her fingers, sprinkling the herbs over the bird. She added salt and pepper and, as the final notes of the *Family Ties* theme song died, slid the chicken into the oven.

Then she turned off the TV, grabbed a rag and started to scrub.

So bite me, she thought. *It helps me think.*

Jenny was right about her job. What happened to her dream of being a photographer? When she and Mark had first married, she was just starting out. A creative fire had burned in her belly. Some interesting freelance assignments came her way that hinted at a promising career, but once she was married and a mother, Mark wanted her at home. She'd resisted at first, but somehow the jobs petered out until, without even a puff, they completely disappeared.

After the divorce, she'd been happy to get the job at the gallery, but ten years in, it felt like—settling.

The only bright spot that she could see in this whole situation was that now she could spend the summer working on her photography. Maddie's boss Eileen had never supported her work as an artist, but there was another gallery owner, Tori at the Edge, who had expressed interest in her black and white darkroom art.

Maddie threw down the duster and pulled her portfolio out from behind the couch. If she was going to make lemonade, she might as well get started. She'd show Tori her photographs tomorrow.

* * *

The following evening, dusk had fallen and her boss Eileen was long gone when Maddie finally closed the heavy glass gallery door and turned the key in the lock. The neon signs of gallery row reflected in the wet pavement as she fought the stream of people hurrying home from work and headed to Pioneer Square. A historic district popular with tourists, it was a mecca for new galleries like the Edge.

Good name, the Edge. Tori had a knack for marketing. Maddie had never been able to get out there and flog her work. After ten years of putting her dreams on hold, it had only gotten harder as her faith in herself slowly ebbed away.

Time to make a change.

As the downtown hustle fell away and she entered the

relative quiet of the streets around the Square, her boots sounded a determined rhythm on the pavement. The rain had eased to a heavy mist that fogged the streetlights and frizzed her hair. The trees showed a faint haze of green and she could smell spring in the air.

In a week the city would be in full bloom. Other years, she would have had her camera out and been snapping atmospheric nighttime shots as she walked. Lately though, the city had lost its magic, and tonight her mind was focused on her meeting with Tori.

Rounding a corner, Maddie's heart lurched at the outline of a hunched figure on a dark storefront step. Tucked in out of the rain, a woman sat with an upturned hat on the ground in front of her.

Time slowed and the ground felt like quicksand beneath Maddie's feet. *Please, no.*

The woman turned to face her. It wasn't her mother. The hand squeezing Maddie's heart loosened its grip and she blew out a sharp breath. Taking a bill from her purse, she dropped it into the hat. "Get yourself something hot to eat," she said gently, even though she knew the chance of that was virtually nil.

As she walked away, her shoulders twitched as she tried to shake off the adrenalin buzz. Now that her mother lived in the city, in the back of her mind Maddie knew that Cindy could pop out anytime, anywhere, and turn Maddie's world upside down.

Suddenly she was standing under Tori's hand-carved gallery sign. Time to get back on track.

She prided herself on being fearless, most of the time. But this one-two punch of her two worst fears, meeting her mother by surprise and showing her photographs to a gallery, had turned her knees to mush. She forced the thoughts of her mother out of her mind—*that wasn't her, just a sad old woman*—and pulled her thoughts back to the job ahead.

Showing her photographs always felt like she was stripped naked and flattened on the gallery wall. She closed her eyes and breathed deeply. *In, one, two. Out, one, two...*

She'd read about this breathing technique in a magazine. It was designed to ease panic attacks and, she discovered while reading the article, apparently she had them.

By the time she reached ten, her heart rate had slowed. Pulling a tube of crimson lipstick out of her shoulder bag, she applied it with a sure hand. The ritual always gave her courage, allowing her to channel the kick-ass, take-no-prisoners femme fatales from the black and white movies she loved.

She rolled her shoulders. *Showtime.* Tugging open the wooden door, she climbed the steep gallery stairs, the envelope with her prints clutched in one clammy hand.

The smell of fresh paint rolled down to greet her and she stopped at the top of the stairs to admire the dark red paint, the color of borsht, that Tori had applied to the walls in preparation for the next show. "Wow."

A muffled voice called out through an open door at the back of the room. "Somebody there?"

Shaking the raindrops off her jacket, Maddie crossed the gallery and peeked into the office. Tori's ample rear end, sheathed in leopard-skin pants, stood in bold relief as she bent over a stack of paintings.

Maddie smiled. "Busy?"

Tori stood up and shook her head, her short pixie-cut hair sticking out in all directions, as usual. "Tuesday night is Art Walk and we're going to be swamped. Not that I'm complaining." Her gaze dropped to the envelope in Maddie's hands and her face lit up. "For me?"

Nerves hit the panic button in Maddie's brain and her fingers instinctively tightened on the envelope. Tori tugged it out of her hands with a wicked grin and spread the gritty eight-by-ten black and whites of the city and its people out on the table.

"These are fantastic. Great contrast. Your darkroom work adds so much drama; I just want to rub my finger over those velvety blacks. People are eager for black and whites again. They're tired of photoshopped specials."

Maddie's shoulders relaxed. It was going to be fine.

Then Tori asked, "Weren't these in your show last year?"

Maddie's chin came up, her eyes widened. "You saw the show?" That venue had been more of a gift shop, not a real gallery at all.

"I read the article in *The Caller* and stopped by."

Maddie nodded, her mind racing. "It brought in a lot of people. I only have a few pieces left. I was hoping you could put them up sometime."

Tori shook her head. "I don't know kiddo." She tapped the prints on the table in front of her. "These are great, but they're old work. I was hoping you'd bring me something new."

Gritting her teeth, Maddie attempted to smile. That was a problem. She didn't have any new work. Shortly after last winter's show, somehow, somewhere, she'd lost her muse. The urban shots on which she'd built her reputation—such as it was—didn't inspire her anymore. The spark had died leaving her a gutted candle, a hollow puddle of wax. She had hoped getting a few pictures into a gallery would give her the push she needed to start moving in a fresh direction. Tori was right though. She couldn't put up old work.

Maddie gathered the prints into a pile. "I understand."

Tori fisted her hands on her sturdy hips. "I don't think you do. You need to get your ass out from behind that counter at Eileen's and get behind the camera where you belong. These are great, but it's time you had your own show. Right here. My October artist just cancelled. Can I pencil you in?"

Maddie's eyes widened. Her own show. *Her*work up on the walls. The chance of a lifetime. The star falls and breaks her leg and Maddie Tedesco steps in.

But October was only six months away. Could she possibly get a new body of work together by then while still working full time? Eileen would hit the ceiling...

But what about her resolution to be a better role model for Jenny? Wasn't the best way to go after what *she* wanted, too?

Although Tori was several inches shorter than Maddie, she managed to put her arm around Maddie's shoulders. "You know, sometimes to get the good things in life you have to take a leap of faith. Like I did last year when I opened this gallery."

Maddie heard Elyse Keaton's voice whisper in her ear. *Time to make lemonade, dear.*

Okay. She grabbed the last lemon and squeezed.

"I'll take the show."

"Good, I'll pencil you in."

"No. You can write it in pen. I'm not sure if I'm jumping or if I've been pushed, but I'm definitely taking the show."

* * *

Elbows on the kitchen table, Maddie rested her head in her hands, the bass rhythm from the floor below beating a backbeat to her thoughts.

What was she thinking, accepting Tori's offer? How could she take the show?

How could she not?

Even after she and Mark had split up, she had continued taking pictures. Preferring the compositional challenge of black and white, she had set up her darkroom in the bathroom, taking Jenny inside when she was too young to be left in the apartment alone.

But Jenny was almost grown now, taken care of for the

summer, and this show—*a solo show*—had dropped in her lap. How could she pass it up? Especially with the long, lonely, rest-of-her-life looming ahead of her. This was her chance to get back in the game.

If she was being perfectly honest, she knew why she'd stayed working for Eileen for so long. It was safe. Secure. Didn't demand she put herself on the line. Now, though, she was afraid she had traded that safety for her daughter's respect, and lost her own creative spark along the way.

That was something Mark had never understood, that to her photography was like breathing. It was how she experienced the world and without it, she only felt half alive. She might as well just breathe into the top half of her lungs, never feeling the satisfaction of filling them completely. Without her photography as an outlet, numbness had slowly crept into her extremities.

Outside her tiny kitchen window, the setting sun gilded the snowy mountain tops that peeked up from behind the downtown. She'd never been to the Olympic Peninsula before. Had never had the time or money for any kind of holiday. She needed something to jumpstart her creative juices though. And leaving the city and heading into the mountains? That would be different. That would be new. Surely then she would find her muse.

Take the summer off to work on the show? That was crazy. Wasn't it? Could she afford it? Maybe just barely.

This would be something truly worthwhile to spend her nest egg on. An investment in herself, in her future. A fresh start.

If she was going to make the most of this chance, she couldn't hold back. She had to be all in.

Chapter 2

Three weeks later to the day, Maddie dropped Jenny at Mark's house to finish the school year. Eileen had hit the gallery's vaulted ceiling when Maddie told her she wanted to take the summer off to work on the show, but once Maddie found an art student to fill in for the season, things had tumbled into place. As if the universe was giving her a big thumbs-up. She just crossed her fingers that her job would be waiting for her when she got back.

As she pulled away from Mark's house, father and daughter stood on the stone front steps, waving goodbye, Mark's arm draped casually over Jenny's shoulder. Maddie watched them recede in the rear-view mirror and—*oh, great*—Mark's new wife Kate joined them on the steps. The stone front steps of the beautiful heritage house they had lovingly restored. The perfect family in the perfect house. Maddie shook her head and dragged her eyes back to the road. How could she ever compete with that?

Two hours later, Maddie stood on the deck of the giant car ferry as it plowed across Puget Sound. Her Nikon digital to her eye, she zoomed in on the forested slopes of the Olympic Peninsula as sunlight caught the rugged, snowy peaks. She snapped a shot.

The salt air whipped around her, clearing away all doubt. *This is why I came. This is what I am looking for.* Her new muse was a forest nymph. She just knew it.

But she needed a cheap place to rent for four months, because she planned to be back in the city by Labor Day to work at the gallery and welcome Jenny home. Assuming her daughter wanted to come home after, as Jenny had put it, her "summer in paradise."

That was what worried Maddie most, that Jenny would decide to live with her father. She had to win back her daughter's respect and that meant making good on the show.

It had been years since she'd been on her own. It felt exhilarating—and weird like she had lost her anchor with no timeline to follow and no one to look after. Adrift and disoriented, she needed a home base and she needed it soon. With high hopes and a few apartment leads in her pocket, she drove her aging station wagon, fondly known as The Beast, off the ferry in Bremerton.

Two days later, still looking but starting worry, Maddie pulled into the lot of a fast food diner. None of the places she'd looked at were at all possible. All lacked any hint of inspiration and, in some cases, even basic hygiene. This was no closer to her forest nymph than Seattle.

Tapping an agitated rhythm on the Arborite tabletop, she studied the map. Roads circled the Olympic Peninsula close to the shore with a few smaller roads heading up the river valleys into the mountains.

Further inland was probably less expensive, an important consideration since in the end, unable to bear the thought of other people using their dishes and sleeping in their beds, she hadn't sub-let the Seattle apartment. Online from home, she hadn't seen any inland rentals but maybe she could find a cottage somewhere. Nothing fancy, just a place to sleep, a small kitchen, and a bathroom where she could set up her darkroom.

She could see it in her mind's eye—nestled in the forest, dripping with atmosphere.

A young waitress stopped at her table, pad in hand. "Road trip?"

"Sort of. If you could go anywhere on the peninsula for a holiday, where would you go?"

The girl chewed the end of her pencil, then stabbed a

finger at a lake in the center of the map. "Fortune Bay on Majestic Lake. It's beautiful, right in the mountains. My uncle has a hunting camp there and I go up sometimes in the summer. I love it. He's right on the lake."

Maddie ordered a burger and studied the map. Fortune Bay was a dot on the map at the end of the road running up one side the lake. Isolated, probably rustic and picturesque as all get out. As good a place to start as any.

She ate quickly, then climbed back into the Beast and headed west.

An hour later, she crested a ridge and pulled into a rest stop at the top of the pass. Majestic Lake hugged the curves of the valley below, surrounded by forested mountains, some still tipped in snow, that rolled out to the horizon. Pulse racing, she pulled out her camera, first taking wide-angle shots, then zooming in on the shore.

Goosebumps prickled on her arms. Something down there pulled her like a magnet.

Back in the car, she flew down the mountain and through the town of Majestic, following the signs toward Fortune Bay. Fifteen minutes later, all spent driving through a dark forest worthy of the Brothers Grimm, the lake winked at her again through the trees and, soon after that, a sign welcomed her to Fortune Bay.

Maddie drove slowly though the town; a handful of streets lined with faded, crayon-colored houses and, at the end, a general store. The road continued along the lake from there, in and out of forest and field until, a mile out of town, the trees opened up and a fallow field, bordered by tall evergreens, ran down to the lake.

A cabin peeked through the trees, the crumbling chimney stretching toward the sun as if preening for her attention. Maddie's foot hit the brake and the Beast shuddered to a halt. She inched ahead to the spot where a lane disappeared into the trees and pulled over to the side of the road. From here, the building was hidden in the forest but a hand-painted sign nailed to the trunk of a massive fir tree announced that the cabin was for rent. Someone had written a phone number across the bottom of the sign but, having been disappointed before, she decided it couldn't hurt to take a peek before she called.

She jumped out of the car, ducked under the rope strung across the drive and headed down the lane. A gusty breeze swirled branches overhead and the air had the faintly medicinal tang of lake water and cedar.

At the end of the drive the cabin was waiting, with weathered white siding, an overgrown flowerbed and a porch facing the lake thirty feet away. The wind blew white caps out on the bay and rocked the limbs of the towering evergreens protecting the cabin. Maddie framed a shot of the porch in the viewfinder and clicked.

It was perfect. Charming and oozing with inspiration. She pressed her lips together in excitement. She had found her muse, but could she afford it?

Up on the porch, a sun-bleached couch stood under a picture window and, cupping her hands to the glass, she peered inside. The room was dark. Dead flies lined the sill. Definitely deserted and possibly right in her price range.

Then something moved at the back of the room. Something big.

Maddie stifled a scream and leaped back off the couch, landing on her butt on the wooden porch floor.

The inner door flew open and a man stood in the doorway.

"Looking for something?" he asked, his voice deep and rumbly. He held a work-gloved hand out to help her, but Maddie was already scrambling to her feet.

"Sorry. I thought the cabin was empty."

"It is." He crossed his arms over his chest, his shoulders taking up most of the doorway. Dark hair hung long on his forehead and his eyes, a startling color as bright as the blue dome over the lake, set off faint warning bells in her head.

For a moment she forgot why she was there. Then he raised an eyebrow.

Right. "Is the cabin for rent?"

"It is now. I was just cleaning up. It's been empty, but some kids got in—were partying inside. We're lucky they didn't burn the place down. That's why we decided to rent."

A gust of wind pushed Maddie like hands on her back towards the door until they were standing face to face. "Can I look inside?"

He stepped out of her way and waved her in.

A tattered doormat *kaflumped* in place sending up a cloud of sun-spangled dust. Looking down, she read the script on the mat, *Welcome Home*, and smiled as she stepped inside.

Most of the cabin could be seen at a glance; one large room with the kitchen on the left and the living room on the right. Through an opening at the back she glimpsed a bedroom, mostly hidden by a flowery curtain hanging in the doorway.

The furniture was old and well used but would do just fine. A calendar, six years out of date, hung on the wall beside a shelf lined with figurines of dancing women. Dust was thick on every surface but the place smelled clean and fresh—she sniffed—almost sweet.

It was perfect.

She returned to the porch but the man had gone down to stand by the water, looking out over the bay with his cell phone to his ear. When he heard her come out, he put the phone in his back pocket and walked up to the cabin.

As Maddie hurried down the steps to meet him, the bottom step rocked and she stumbled. He reached out and grabbed her arm—letting her go almost at once when she regained her balance.

She stood perfectly still, pulse racing, her heart beating double time, the imprint of his hand still warm on her arm. *No harm, no foul.*

"I'll fix that," he said. "So are you interested?"

"How much?"

"Four hundred a month, two months in advance. As is. Water's on. Everything works."

"I'll take it. And I'll pay cash. Could I have a receipt?"

"Sure," he said and went into the cabin.

Maddie spun around, her back to the cabin door, and felt around in the bottom of her shoulder bag until her hand closed on a soft lumpy shape. Her money sock, her nest-egg, all the money she had in the world. She liked to have it close, just in case.

She pulled a roll of bills the size of her fist out of the sock, much of it earned at the show last year, and wincing, peeled sixteen fifties off the roll. It was a big chunk of cash, but compared to sleeping in motel rooms and eating in diners, the cabin was a bargain.

The man came back onto the porch, a pad in his hand, pen at the ready. "My name's Jake Murphy. Phone number's on the receipt. And you are?"

"Maddie Tedesco."

She spelled out her last name and he wrote it on the pad, then they exchanged the money for the receipt.

"Where are you from?"

"Seattle."

"How long are you planning to stay?"

"For the summer."

He handed her a key on a brass chain that pooled cool as water in the palm of her hand.

Her eyes widened and she shrugged. "That's it?" She had expected a lot more red tape. References at the very least.

"I know where you live," he said, one side of his mouth

twitching back in a half-smile that popped a dimple on his lean, whiskered cheek.

She pressed her lips firmly together. That dimple could definitely be a problem. But before she could ruminate on that any further, he was gone, raising a hand in salute as he disappeared around the corner of the cabin.

Maddie closed her hand around the key and did a silent fist pump in the air. *Yes.* She'd found her home base.

The Beast was still out on the road, but first things first—to find the bathroom.

There weren't many places to look. A steep staircase without a railing at the back of the kitchen led to a trap door in the ceiling. She hoped it wasn't up there—the attic was probably full of mice, or worse.

Lifting the flowered curtain, she surveyed the bedroom. Bed, dresser, a time-speckled mirror. Lifting the lid of a large cedar trunk in the corner, she saw it was full of clean linens that smelled sweet, like the rest of the cabin, of vanilla and spice. Surprising considering it looked like the place had been empty for years.

She pulled a quilt out of the trunk. Like something a grandmother would make, the fabric felt soft against her cheek and she inhaled the safe, clean smell of cedar. For a moment her eyes drifted shut. Forcing them open she shook her head. She'd make the bed later but first, the bathroom.

Where could it be? The cabin was small—unless …

She sucked in a horrified breath. What if she'd rented a place with an outhouse?

Back on the porch, she scanned the woods for a shed with a sickle moon on the door.

Nothing. Then she noticed a shorter than normal door at the end of the porch. Feeling a little like Alice, she turned the knob and stepped into an antiquated laundry room. Another door faced her on the far wall and she opened it cautiously, her mind reeling back to thoughts of mice and worse. To her relief, there was a small but complete bathroom inside. A broken, boarded-up window stood over a claw-foot tub, but otherwise, as advertised, everything worked.

She used the facilities, running her hand longingly along the tub's cool porcelain lip on her way out. A hot soak would have to wait.

Pulling the Beast up beside the cabin, she carried everything inside and shut the door. May was cold in the mountains, and the cabin, surrounded by trees, received little direct sunlight at this time of year. Wrapping her arms around her ribs for warmth, she searched the walls for a thermostat. Instead she came face to face with a woodstove in the corner.

She groaned. *How did I miss that little detail?*

"Unpack first, deal with the woodstove later," she said aloud, then shook her head. "Talking to myself already and only four more months to go."

She put the map of the Peninsula up on the living room wall and plugged in an old TV in a big wooden cabinet that stood in the corner behind the front door. She didn't expect color but was dismayed when all she got was static.

Of course there wasn't cable. Or wifi. She'd have to figure something out if she was going to work on her website because that was the other prong of her new career strategy—to design a website to market the thousands of digital photographs of Seattle she'd taken to magazines and online travel sites.

Carefully, she arranged her framed photographs of Jenny on top of the old TV, wondering if she could stay busy enough to not miss her daughter.

She unpacked her clothes and made the bed, then fished the money sock out of her purse. Getting down on her knees, she stashed it safely at the back of the bottom dresser drawer.

When she returned to the kitchen, the mountains across the lake were a dark silhouette against a fading turquoise sky. Her darkroom equipment still lay in a pile on the living room floor; enlarger, plastic trays, jugs of chemicals and boxes of paper. It would all have to wait until morning.

She switched on the lights and shivered as the cold settled into her bones. Finding a heavy plaid jacket hung behind the door, she tugged it on and turned to the woodstove in the corner.

Should have done this first thing. A roaring blaze would chase out the cold that clung to the walls. She'd seen firewood piled neatly in the driveway, so she marched outside and picked out a round log the diameter of her thigh. Back inside, she scrunched up some paper, put it in the stove, set the log on top and struck a match.

The match flamed, the paper caught, the fire flare brightly—then burned out. The log sat untouched on a bed of ash.

Maddie tried again, using more paper and a pile of wood scraps from the pail behind the stove. A few minutes later smoke poured out the open iron door but this time a faint waft of heat drift up.

Pretty darn proud of herself, she swung the heavy door shut and brushed the soot off her hands. She looked around and nodded. She could do this. Just stick to the plan. She always had a master plan. It was how she kept her life on track. The current plan was: take the pictures, get Jenny back, then mount the show. Definitely do-able. Moving on with her life.

Suddenly exhausted, she made a quick dinner of the bread and peanut butter she'd had in the car. Then she hung the jacket on the back of the bedroom chair, kicked off her shoes and fell into bed, pulling up the soft quilt up under her chin.

Sometimes, in times of stress, she felt more comfortable sleeping in her clothes. Old habits die hard, the cabin was cold, and she didn't have to justify her actions to anyone.

Besides, you never knew when, in a strange place, you might have to run.

Chapter 3

Thwack. Maddie's eyes flew open. Sound waves reverberated up the bed's iron legs, making the bedsprings vibrate.

Thwack.

Throwing off the blankets, she jumped out of bed, squealing when her feet hit the icy linoleum. A dark head passed by the window. Maddie dropped to her knees, scrambled to the window and pulled herself up at the sill.

Jake stood in the driveway, an axe in his hand. Setting a round, stove-length log on a stump, he brought the axe down with tremendous force. Maddie's eyebrows shot up as wood went flying.

He bent to pick up another log and set it on the stump. Then, *Thwack!* Shoulders rippling, he split that piece in two.

Have mercy. She'd never known a man who could swing an axe before—or one who'd even tried. He flipped a log upright with the toe of his boot and split it right there where it stood on the ground with another powerful stroke.

I've got to get a picture of that.

Her eyes glued to the action outside, Maddie patted her chest. Thank goodness she was already dressed. Grabbing the plaid jacket from the chair and her camera from the table, she headed for the door.

* * *

Jake wiped the sweat from his forehead. *Already warming up.*

The new tenant stumbled out onto the porch, pulling on a jacket—*his* jacket. Her eyes were still puffy with sleep and stray wisps of hair caught the sunlight as it curled every-which-way.

He'd always liked that tousled, just-got-out-of-bed kind of look. A smile tugged the corner of his mouth. "Morning."

"Morning." She squinted, obviously trying to get her mind in gear. "What are you doing?"

"Splitting firewood. It won't burn like this."

Aware of her watching, he set another piece of wood on the stump and brought down the axe, foolishly pleased by how neatly it split.

He turned back to find her aiming a big camera his way. She snapped a quick shot. "Hope you don't mind."

"Guess not," he said, but frowned, not entirely sure.

She watched him for a moment with those sleepy eyes as he set another round of wood on the stump, then she retreated into the cabin.

What *was* he doing here? Good question. Sure, things needed doing around the place, but whatever happened to keeping his distance?

The axe came down hard.

He had rules about women, and a woman from the city living so close to the farm was way outside his safety zone. But the nights were still cold, she was his tenant and, from the look of her, had never split a piece of firewood in her life.

Thwack. More pieces went flying. Slowly the tension in his shoulders eased. He'd always enjoyed the rhythmic sound and motion of splitting wood.

Gotta get more exercise.

* * *

Ten minutes later, Maddie walked out of the cabin feeling more in control, a steaming cup of coffee in each hand.

She watched as Jake leaned the axe against the house and rolled his shoulders loosely, like a cat. Then in one smooth motion he stripped off his grey woolen sweater to reveal a tight black T-shirt underneath that clearly defined the carved contours of his torso. What she'd give to get a picture of *that,* too. But she'd seen the way he looked at the camera and didn't want to press her luck. Not yet.

Jake turned to her and raised one eyebrow.

Her brain stalled for a moment, then she remembered the cups in her hands and thrust one toward him. "Sorry. It's black. I don't have any milk or sugar yet."

"Thanks. This'll be fine." As he reached for the cup, his blue eyes swept over her, the hint of a smile sparking that damn dimple again.

Maddie took a quick scalding gulp of her coffee, watching him over the rim.

He tested the rocky step with one battered work boot. "I'll get to this."

"No rush."

He took a sip of coffee and looked around the yard, seemingly content with the silence that followed.

Maddie was never comfortable with silence. It felt like an itch she had to scratch. She sipped, shifted her weight, her brain screaming, *say something.*

"I'm a photographer."

She hadn't meant to say *that.*

"Really."

She nodded. More silence. Grinding her teeth, she took another sip.

Jake cleared his throat. "Going to take some pictures around here?"

"Yes. I hope to."

I hope to? Where did *that* come from?

"Well, good luck." He glanced at his watch, gulped down his coffee and handed her the empty mug. "Thanks. I've gotta go."

Grabbing his sweater off the woodpile, he hung the axe

on a nail on the wall and said, "I'll chop some more when I get a chance." Then he turned and strode up the long leafy drive, sweater slung over his shoulder, his lean frame in motion a joy to watch.

She couldn't suppress a sigh. Then shook her head and grinned. *Stop that right now.* The last thing she needed was a complication like that. With her show coming up and Jenny to see to, she didn't need any complications right now. Anyway, she was better off on her own, making her own decisions and sticking to her own plans.

She bent to pick up an armload of split wood.

Don't wish for something you can't have. Relationships were too risky for people like her. The only thing she knew about 'family' was what she'd learned on TV, and she was pretty sure that wasn't enough to make it work.

She cast one last look down the empty lane. But those blue eyes and that dimple when he smiled? That man was going to be trouble.

And "good luck." What exactly did he mean by that?

* * * * *

You can find *Summer of Fortune*
and the other Fortune Bay books in e-book, paperback and audio book format through my website,

www.JudithHudsonAuthor.com

Or find me on **Facebook** at

Judith Hudson - Author

Also by Judith Hudson

The Secret at Elk Horn Lodge

The Fortune Bay Romance Series:

Lake of Dreams

Summer of Fortune

The Good Neighbor

Home for Christmas

Family Matters

Starting Over

Starlight and Tinsel

By J. M. Hudson

The Rocky and Bernadette Mystery Series

Temple of the Jaguar
A travel cozy mystery.

A travel writer and a photographer's first job together in the Yucatan quickly unravels when a body is discovered in the crocodile lagoon.

Murder in the Piazza
Coming 2022

Thanks to my daughter Rosey Hudson for the help, as always. A yoga retreat aficionado that she is, for the idea of yoga instructor as a career path for our sweetly counter-culture Star.

Thanks to my friend and editor Stephanie Webb for always being there to talk over plot points, and for adding so much to this book. And to Ann, Mara and Susheela for the proofreads.

Copyright

Starlight and Tinsel is a work of fiction. Names, characters, places and incidents are entirely the product of the imagination of the author or are used fictitiously. Any resemblance to actual events, locales or persons, living or dead, is entirely coincidental.

Published by Tall Trees Books, November 2018

ISBN: 978-1-7752022-8-8